THE WANDERING BEGGAR

THE WANDERING

BEGGAR... OR THE

ADVENTURES OF SIMPLE SHMEREL

AS TOLD BY SOLOMON SIMON

ILLUSTRATED BY LILLIAN FISCHEL

BEHRMAN HOUSE, INC., PUBLISHERS • NEW YORK, 1955

Published by

BEHRMAN HOUSE, INC.

1261 BROADWAY, NEW YORK

MANUFACTURED IN THE UNITED STATES OF AMERICA

To Lena

CONTENTS

vii

THE WANDERING BEGGAR

Simple Shmerel

A LONG TIME AGO THERE LIVED A man and his wife and their seven sons. Six of them were clever and handsome, but the seventh, alas, was an ugly, stupid fellow whose name was Shmerel. His poor father and mother didn't know what to do with him—whatever they told him went in one ear and out the other; whatever they taught him, he promptly forgot.

The children of the village were forever teasing him. They made faces at him and called him names. "Blockhead! Moonface! Ninny!" they would shout. And every name they called him stuck like glue. Shmerel would become wild with anger, grab a stick or a stone and chase after them. Then the children would run and hide in a doorway or behind a fence and chant tauntingly:

> *Simple Shmerel,*
> *Tall and thin.*
> *Head's a pumpkin,*
> *Brain's a pin!*

1

Poor Shmerel would burst into tears and run crying to his mother.

"Stop your snivelling," she would scold. "Don't be such a fool and they won't make fun of you."

"But what'll I do?"

"Be like your brothers."

"B-u-t I c-a-n-'-t."

His mother would dry his tears with the corner of her apron and sigh, "Oh, what's to become of you! What's to become of you!"

Years passed. Shmerel grew and grew till he became big and square as a block of stone and strong as a chunk of iron; but his face was still simple and child-like, with puzzled, frightened eyes.

"What are we to do with him?" the poor couple wailed.

"Send him out into the world," the townsfolk said. "Let him rub shoulders with all kinds of people. Maybe then some of his simplicity will be rubbed off."

So his father and mother scraped and saved, and saved and scraped, and bought Shmerel a new suit of clothes, a pair of shiny, new shoes and a bright new cap. Night after night, his mother darned his stockings and mended his shirts. Then, one fine spring morning, they sent their son out into the great, wide world.

"Good luck, Simple Shmerel," they cried.

2

The Three Thieves

HMEREL WANDERED AIMLESSLY FROM village to village, from town to town, and from city to city. His fine, new coat had long since turned to tatters, his once sturdy shoes had worn out long before and now his feet were wrapped in rags; his cap was torn and full of holes. His face was wrinkled and his beard dirty and unkempt. He carried a sack over his shoulder and a thick staff in his hand. He had become just a hunched-over, cringing beggar.

So Shmerel wandered for six years. In the seventh year, he came to a great city. He was hungry and tired and dragged his heavy feet through the clean, cobbled streets. But here Shmerel was afraid to beg because he had already learned that the rich don't like the poor. With his cap pulled low over his face and his eyes looking humbly at the ground, he hurried past the splendid homes of the city burghers.

At last he came to the dark and narrow streets of the poor, and there, in sing-song fashion, he plaintively chanted the beggars' ditty he had learned long before.

3

Good people, kind people, have pity on me!
Listen to a starving beggar's plea:
Alms, alms, a penny, a crust of bread—
"Feed the hungry," the Lord has said.

Simple Shmerel finished his song and stood still, waiting for the piece of stale bread or the copper penny that people sometimes threw out to him. But this time, much to his surprise, a door was opened and the master of the house reverently invited him to come in. Shmerel quickly stepped inside, without noticing the crowd that immediately began to gather around the house.

His host led Shmerel to the dining-room. Here he seated him at the head of the table and set a good meal before him. Simple Shmerel asked no questions. When they gave him meat, he ate it. When they gave him wine, he drank it. He was no fool when it came to that!

After such a good dinner, he became sleepy. So he just folded his arms on the table, laid his head on his arms, and fell asleep.

"Hush!" whispered his host. "He sleeps."

He slept a long time. When he awoke, he yawned lazily, rubbed his eyes and looked up. Lo! Seven generals, shining in gold braid and silver buttons, stood straight as bow-strings before him. When their chief saw that Shmerel had awakened, he bowed low and said:

4

"O great and holy man! We have been sent to you by His Highness, the Prince. May we find favor in your eyes. Come with us to the castle. A great evil has befallen us. The treasure-house of the Prince has been robbed and the most learned astrologers and the greatest magicians have not been able to discover the thieves. Only you, Porush the Seer, can help us. A guard of honor is waiting without to accompany you to the castle. Come with us."

Simple Shmerel did not know that they had mistaken him for Porush the Seer, the famous Holy Man, who often traveled about disguised as a beggar. Indeed, the officer's long and flowery address puzzled Simple Shmerel. All he understood were the words, "Come with us," and when silver buttons command, one must obey.

So Simple Shmerel went with them to the castle of the Prince. In front, marched the seven generals in their gold-braided uniforms. After them stumbled Simple Shmerel. Then followed seventeen solemn courtiers wearing high silk hats and seventy-seven hussars on bright black stallions. Behind the hussars, in perfect formation, marched four hundred and forty-four foot soldiers with drawn swords.

Simple Shmerel was frightened. His teeth chattered, his knees knocked together. "What will all the soldiers do to me?"

The procession reached the castle. The gates swung open. The ladies of the court crowded the balconies and ran down the steps to welcome the Holy Man. The Prince himself came out to meet him.

"Do you wish for anything, Holy Man?" asked the Prince.

Hungry Shmerel had but one answer to such a question. So, once again, he sang out:

Good people, kind people, have pity on me!
Listen to a starving beggar's plea:
Alms, alms, a penny, a crust of bread—
"Feed the hungry," the Lord has said.

"A dinner for the Holy Man!" commanded the Prince.

They brought him broiled tongues of nightingales and stewed hearts of pheasants, a great bowl of turtle soup, baked chicken and roast duck, all kinds of pies and tarts, and bottles of spiced wine. Simple Shmerel ate and drank and drank and ate until he began to feel sleepy. Then the Prince led him to one of the bedrooms of the palace. Here Shmerel stretched himself on the great, soft feather-bed and quickly fell asleep.

"Quiet!" commanded the Prince. "The Holy Man, Porush the Seer, sleeps. Quiet!"

Simple Shmerel snored.

Meanwhile, in the quiet of the kitchen, in a corner near the big brick stove, three servants whispered anxiously together. They were the thieves who had robbed the Prince's treasure-house and had buried the silver, the gold, and the precious jewels beneath an apple tree in the orchard.

They were worried, for it was said that Porush the Seer, the Holy Man, could see through the thickest wall and they were afraid that he would surely find the hidden treasure. They shuddered at the thought of the fate that awaited them. They would be put in chains, thrown into the dungeon, and then hanged.

"Listen, you fools!" said the oldest and boldest of the

8

three thieves. "There's no need to be frightened. If we were smart enough to break into the Prince's treasure-chamber under his very nose and to rob him in spite of the heavy guard, we can surely outwit this Holy Seer. Let one of us hide under Porush's bed and watch his every move. When we see that he's discovered where the treasure is hidden, we'll hide it somewhere else."

"A good idea," agreed the two other thieves.

"And now," said the oldest robber to the youngest, "go hide under Porush's bed."

"Why pick on me?" protested the youngest thief. "I didn't do anything. I only broke the locks and drugged the watchman. *You* go. It was your idea in the first place."

"Very well, then," said the oldest. "Let us draw lots."

So they drew lots and the oldest thief saw to it that it fell to the youngest to hide under Shmerel's bed.

Simple Shmerel awoke, yawned luxuriously, and gazed about him in contentment. A butler served afternoon tea. Shmerel drank it strong and well-sweetened and munched many cookies with it. Then he wiped his mouth with the back of his hand and decided to take a stroll through the palace.

He walked slowly, his hands behind his back, humming a tune. He didn't know what to do with himself. He entered the library where he saw high walls lined with books, and became curious. He knew that clever and learned people were always looking into books.

"I'll take a look, too," he thought.

He took a book from a shelf, opened it, and stared at the black print and the white paper. He didn't understand a word of it, for he had never learned how to read. He threw the book on the floor in disgust. A servant immediately stooped to pick it up. Shmerel took up another book, glanced at a page, and then threw it, too, upon the floor. Another servant stooped down and picked that one up too.

Simple Shmerel liked this new game. He reached up to a shelf and took down an armful of richly gilded books. He flipped one book open, glanced at a page, and threw it on the floor with a thud. When he was finished with the first load of books, he took another armful from the shelves. The servants carefully picked the books up as fast as he threw them down.

A courtier hurried to the Prince with the important news. "Porush the Seer is searching for something in all the books and he can't find it."

"Bring him more books!" the Prince commanded. "Bring him every book in the castle. Porush the Seer must find what he is searching for!"

Simple Shmerel treated the new books as he had the

old, and, always, the servants trooped after him, picking up the books from the floor.

"What will he do next?" they gasped.

Suddenly Shmerel stopped the game. Among the thick, heavy volumes they had brought him, there was, by chance, a picture-book for children—a square, thin, red book. This book pleased Shmerel very much. He took it in his hands and held it in front of him for a long time, admiring its bright red color. All the servants held their breath. Something was going to happen!

Shmerel tucked the book under his arm happily, went back to his room, and sat down on the soft sofa opposite the bed. He opened the book, and began thumbing through the pages. Now he could see why all learned people like books. Such pretty pictures, such bright colors! He smiled to himself.

"Now this is a book!" he thought.

He turned the colored pages slowly, staring attentively at each picture. Suddenly he stopped. Look! A beautiful big black dog spotted with white was lying stretched out on the ground with his head between his forepaws and his eyes half closed. Shmerel looked at the picture and muttered to himself. "How beautiful! Just like a real, live dog!"

Simple Shmerel looked and looked. . . . That he might see the better, he shut one eye and squinted at the picture with his other eye, as though he were looking through a spy-glass. It seemed to him that the dog was really alive, and that it had just now fallen asleep in the heat of the midday sun. So Shmerel waited patiently. He wanted to see how long a dog could lie so still and quiet.

He waited five minutes, then ten minutes, fifteen minutes—an hour. The dog didn't bat an eyelash. Simple Shmerel became annoyed. He rose from the sofa with the book in his hand, looked sharply at the dog, and cried out angrily: "Get up, you lazy dog! Get up, you lazy good-for-nothing! Get out of there and stand up, I say! Do you think you can lie there forever?"

The thief lying under the bed was terrified. "My God! What power the Holy Man has!"

Simple Shmerel continued to shout at the dog. "Get out of there and stand up, I say! Do you hear me?"

Trembling, the thief crawled out from under the bed and fell at Shmerel's feet.

"O, Holy Man, have pity on me!" he wailed. "I didn't rob the treasure-house. It was the other two who did it! It was they who buried the silver, the gold, and the precious jewels under the apple tree in the orchard. Have pity on me, Holy Man! I didn't do it. I only broke the locks."

The courtiers attending Shmerel hurried to the Prince

12

with the good news that the Seer had discovered the thieves. And immediately the three servants were caught and thrown into the dungeon in chains.

The Prince loaded Simple Shmerel with precious gifts. Shmerel stuffed them all into his sack and went out into the great, wide world.

Calman's Shadow

JUDAH CALMAN, THE RICH MERCHANT, was a tall and handsome man. His glossy black beard was always neatly trimmed and his clothes were of the very best. His coachman, Zalman, was also a tall and handsome man. Like his master, he had a well-trimmed black beard and dark-brown eyes.

Zalman was a good coachman. He kept Calman's carriage clean and well polished. The hay in the barn was always fresh, the oats were without chaff, and the pails from which the horses drank were always bright and shiny. Zalman was honest, he never drank, and he went to bed early.

He had but one fault: he was always imitating his master. He even mimicked his master's walk and manner. When Judah Calman walked, he would clasp his hands behind his back; so Zalman, the coachman, would walk with his hands behind his back, too. When Judah Calman talked, he would keep one eye half closed, so Zalman, too, would talk with one eye half shut, as though watching

14

something very closely. When the master laughed, he would lift one shoulder a little and, when he argued, he would tilt his head slightly to one side. And in all these things, too, Zalman, the coachman, was just like his master. People would laugh at him and call him "Calman's Shadow."

One summer day, the coachman, Zalman, was driving his master, Judah Calman, through a forest to a far-away city. The day was clear and sunny, and very hot. The horses trotted briskly, setting up a breeze, but it didn't help much. Judah Calman sat in his carriage, his coat and vest unbuttoned, and perspired. He wiped his face with a silk handkerchief. But despite the terrible heat, Judah Calman was cheerful. Business was thriving, and he hummed to himself:

"O hearken to the words of the Lord . . ."

And Zalman sang after him. "O hearken to the words of the Lord . . ."

Judah Calman became annoyed. He changed to . . . "All are equal in the eyes of the Lord . . ."

Zalman repeated word for word: "All are equal in the eyes of the Lord . . ."

Judah Calman became more annoyed. He stopped singing. The coachman also stopped singing. After a while, Calman sighed heavily to himself. "What a day, what a day. Such heat!"

"What a day, what a day. Such heat!" sighed Zalman after him. Judah Calman lost patience.

"Stop mimicking me, fool!" he shouted angrily at his coachman. "My God, did you ever hear the like of it? Just as everyone says—my shadow!"

Zalman grew red with shame, but didn't say anything.

Judah had become even more uncomfortable and hot in his excitement. He turned to Zalman. "Look sharp!" he said gruffly. "There must be a brook around here where I can bathe."

"Not far, master."

"How far, stupid one?"

"About two miles, master."

"Good! Stop using your tongue, parrot, and begin using your whip!"

"Yes, master." And Zalman lashed the horses.

They soon came to the brook. Zalman reined in the horses and Judah Calman climbed out of the carriage. He found a place well screened by bushes, undressed, and waded into the water.

The merchant swam and floated in the cool water for a long time. When he was through, he hurried to the bushes where he had left his clothes. They weren't there! He went deeper into the bushes, looked about, searched carefully, but could find no trace of them. All he found were some old clothes that weren't his, but looked like Zalman's. So he shouted:

"Zalman! Zalman!"

There was no answer. Calman became frightened. Something must have happened to his coachman. "Somebody killed Zalman, stole my clothes, and rode off with the horses!" thought the terrified Calman. He hid in the bushes and listened. There wasn't a sound. He grew calmer.

"There's no sense in going around stark naked," he said to himself. So he put on the clothes that he had found and stole to the road. He saw his horses grazing

17

leisurely. In the carriage sat Zalman, dressed in his master's clothes, smoking a cigarette and blowing smoke rings into the air. Judah Calman grew red with anger.

"Hey, you stupid parrot of a coachman!" he shouted, waving his arms. "What kind of a joke is this? Get out of the carriage! Take off my clothes and put on your own rags! Hitch the horses and let's be off. We should have been on our way an hour ago."

The coachman looked at his master, cocked his head, and said quietly, "Poor Zalman! He's out of his mind. The heat must have affected him. Else how would he dare talk to his master like that?"

"Stupid!" shouted the merchant. "Don't you recognize your own master?"

"I suppose you think you're my master?" smiled his double indulgently.

"Of course I'm your master!" answered Judah Calman impatiently. "Get up to your box and no more nonsense!"

"Tsk, tsk! The heat has affected my coachman," said Zalman, shaking his head sadly.

"Not *I*, but you are affected by the heat, fool!" shouted Judah Calman.

"Let it be so," said Zalman quietly. "You're Judah Calman, the rich merchant. But, meanwhile, hitch the horses and let us be off. We should have been on our way an hour ago."

18

"What? Am *I* to hitch the horses?" asked the startled merchant.

"Who else? And then again—if you don't want to, don't. Stay here. The forest is full of wolves." Zalman smiled.

Judah Calman thought excitedly of overpowering his coachman.

"Well?" said Zalman quietly.

"I'd better wait till we get to the city," thought Judah Calman. He said nothing, but hitched the horses to the carriage and climbed up to the box.

Though late in the afternoon, it was still hot. The horses trotted briskly, setting up a breeze, but it didn't help much. Scowling and whipping the horses, Judah Calman sat hunched on the box while Zalman sprawled on the back seat of the carriage, humming to himself:

"O hearken to the words of the Lord . . ."

He stopped in the middle and began another tune:

"All are equal in the eyes of the Lord . . ."

He didn't finish the second song either. He unbuttoned his vest, stretched himself contentedly, and sighed, "What a day, what a day!"

Judah Calman could endure it no longer. He turned his head and shouted, "Stop it, you fool!"

"What a coachman!" sighed Zalman. "Stop using your tongue and begin using your whip!"

Judah Calman bit his lip and lashed the horses.

They drove on for a day and a night, a night and a day, and on the third day they came to the city. Calman reined in the horses and drove into the courtyard of the first inn they came to. Zalman, dressed as the rich merchant, stepped out of the carriage and briskly commanded Judah Calman to unhitch the horses. But Judah Calman didn't listen to him. He stood up on the box, waved his arms and shouted: "Help! Help! Honest people, help! I've been robbed!"

A big crowd gathered around the carriage and all began clamoring noisily. "When? Where?" they asked. "Who did it?"

Judah Calman pointed his finger at Zalman. "He did it! My coachman!"

The crowd turned to where the stranger was pointing. They saw a well dressed merchant standing quietly on the steps of the inn, looking pitifully at the excited coachman.

"He?" asked someone from the crowd with surprise.

"Yes, he!" Then Calman told his story.

After Calman had finished, Zalman smiled and said: "It looks as if my coachman has gone crazy. It was terribly hot three days ago. The poor fellow was affected by the heat and took to thinking that *he* is Judah Calman and that *I* am his coachman, Zalman. I have papers in my money bag which will identify me."

The people were impressed by Zalman's calm manner. His voice was gentle and assured and he was well dressed. He looked the well-to-do merchant. But Calman continued to scream: "Help, help, honest people! He lies, he lies!"

"Who can tell? Maybe there's something to the coachman's story," shouted someone in the crowd.

"Let's take them to the Rabbi," said another. "Let *him* decide."

Calman and Zalman were both brought before the Rabbi and each told his story. Calman spoke with great excitement while Zalman pretended to be annoyed by the delay. The Rabbi listened to them attentively. His sharp eyes noticed something queer. Both merchant and coachman looked almost alike. Both had the same manner of walking and talking, and even their black beards were trimmed in the same fashion. And he thought to himself: "There's something wrong here. Yes, there's something wrong."

Meanwhile, the crowd became excited. Everyone talked and argued, and everyone took sides. The Rabbi thought and wondered, wondered and thought, but couldn't come to a decision. He looked helplessly at the two men before him.

21

All of a sudden, the monotonous voice of Simple Shmerel was heard through the window.

"Quiet!" someone shouted. "Isn't that the Holy Man?" They all listened.

> *Good people, kind people, have pity on me!*
> *Listen to a starving beggar's plea:*
> *Alms, alms, a penny, a crust of bread—*
> *"Feed the hungry," the Lord has said.*

"Yes, that's the Holy Man" someone said. "I recognize his voice," cried another. "He caught the thieves who robbed our prince! He'll know what to do. Ask him in, Rabbi!" they all shouted.

The Rabbi invited Simple Shmerel to come into the house. The merchant and the coachman repeated their stories for the beggar. Everyone listened attentively and watched Simple Shmerel. Shmerel looked as if he too were absorbed in what the two were saying but, in truth, his mind was elsewhere. The odor of fresh bread floating into the room from the nearby kitchen fascinated him.

After Calman and Zalman had finished, the Rabbi sent them from the room. He turned to Simple Shmerel.

"Who is right, Holy Man?" asked the Rabbi.

"Who is right?" repeated Shmerel blankly.

"That is," said the Rabbi, "who is the coachman and who is the merchant?"

22

Shmerel answered simply. "The coachman is the coachman and the merchant is the merchant."

"But they both claim to be the merchant!"

"That cannot be," said Simple Shmerel emphatically.

"True, it cannot be. One is a pretender. But which one?"

But Simple Shmerel still didn't understand. A merchant is a merchant, and a coachman is a coachman. Everyone knows that! So he said: "Just call them back and ask them. *They'll* know." Then, without waiting, he himself called out in a loud voice: "Hey you, coachman! Come here!"

Zalman, from sheer force of habit, quickly opened the door and answered, "Allright, sir, I'm coming." He saw his mistake at once, but it was too late. Everyone immediately realized that the man dressed up as the merchant was really the coachman.

Judah Calman rewarded Shmerel handsomely. Simple Shmerel stuffed the gold into his beggar's bag and went out into the great, wide world.

Pretty Blumkeh

NCE THERE LIVED A CHARCOAL burner named Booni. He lived in a little house on top of a mountain, far, far away in the woods, with his wife, Sarah, and their beautiful daughter, Blumkeh. Every day, at dawn, the charcoal burner would go down to the woods. There he would fell some trees, pile up the wood, and cover the piles with moist turf, leaving a tiny hole at the top. Then he would set fire to them. The covered piles of wood used to smoulder for months on end until they turned into charcoal.

While Booni cared for the fires in the woods, his wife, Sarah, kept house and prepared the meals. But pretty Blumkeh didn't like to stay at home and help her mother. In the summer time she would run and play the whole day long and would not come home until evening.

Her mother, weary and tired after the day's work, would ask:

"Where have you been all day?"

Blumkeh would toss her head and answer impishly, "Nowhere!"

24

"Are you sure?" said Sarah angrily.

"Well, I did go swimming . . ."

"You know your father told you not to go swimming alone in the lake!"

"What's there to be afraid of?"

"Just wait till I tell him!"

"Leave me alone! I'm hungry! I want supper!"

"I want supper! I'm hungry! That's all you know!"

"Is that so. I can crow like a rooster, I can howl like a wolf, and I can even croak like a frog! Listen—I'm a wolf! Wooooooo!" howled Blumkeh.

"Stop it! Enough! You're making me dizzy! Here's your supper, wolf. But just wait till your father hears of this!"

Blumkeh laughed, "You've never told him yet!"

Sarah stroked the girl's blond hair lovingly.

Each day Blumkeh grew more and more lovely, until she was as lovely as the tiny blue corn flower that grows in the fields of corn. And just as this pretty little flower is hidden away among the great, tall stalks, so was the pretty Blumkeh hidden from the world on the mountain top in the midst of the woods.

One hot summer day, a rich merchant and his son, Sholem, were travelling through the woods. The wagon went slowly along the dusty dirt road, swaying from side to side, father and son nodding sleepily. Suddenly the wagon bumped over a thick root and the jolt awakened the merchant and his son. Sholem saw the lazy, plodding gait of the horses and became annoyed. Crack! went the whip. The horses galloped off. An axle scraped against a tree trunk and snapped in two. The wagon stopped with a crash.

"What a son!" shouted the merchant angrily. "This is what you get for hurrying. Now we're stuck in the middle of the woods." Sholem didn't answer. He unhitched the horses silently, looking helplessly about him. The sun was shining brightly, but only a few rays of light came through the thick, leafy branches. All around them were the dark woods.

Neither said anything. It was quite still. Suddenly they heard a voice in the woods, a girlish voice, singing:

> *Play on your fiddle*
> *And guess this riddle:*
> *Legs, four,*
> *No less—no more.*
> *With no flesh covered—*
> *What is it, beloved?*

The voice stopped as if waiting for an answer, then continued: "Can't you guess? Here's another hint. It has feathers—but it isn't a bird!"

Another pause. "Ha, ha, ha!" laughed the voice. "You can't guess, can you? But it's so simple! It's—a bed! A *bed* has four legs and a *bed* has feathers in the pillows."

Sholem gripped his father's shoulder in fright. The voice went on singing:

> *Play on your fiddle*
> *And guess this riddle:*
> *Taller than a house,*
> *Smaller than a mouse,*
> *Sweet as a candy ball,*
> *Bitter as the taste of gall.*

There was another pause, and then more laughter. "Well? I'm waiting. Can't you guess this one, either? I suppose I shall have to tell you the answer again. It's a *bee!* A bee flies higher than a house, and is smaller than a mouse. A bee's sting is as bitter as gall and its honey is as sweet as candy!"

The voice sounded nearer. Suddenly the merchant and his son saw a young girl coming out of the woods. She was laughing and talking to a squirrel perched on her shoulder.

"Look!" Sholem shouted.

Startled by his cry, the squirrel jumped into a tree and

the girl hid among the bushes. The merchant turned angrily to his son.

"What's the matter now?"

"Didn't you see it, father?"

"See what?"

"The fairy!"

"Fairies!" snorted his father. "He's discovered fairies! I've been travelling through these woods a good thirty years and I've yet to see a fairy." The merchant cupped his hands to his mouth and bellowed: "Hey there, girl, our axle is broken. Do you know where we can get help?"

There was no answer from the woods and the merchant turned to his son, angrier than ever.

"Look what you've done! First you frightened the horses and now you've frightened the girl away!"

A pair of blue eyes peeked out of the bushes. Then a head of golden hair was seen and, at last, in a bright cotton dress came the girl. It was Blumkeh.

"Don't be afraid," said the merchant gently. "We are Jews from the city. Our axle is broken and we haven't an axe with which to fix it. Can you help us?"

Blumkeh didn't answer, but she beckoned as if to say, "Come!" They followed her until they came to the charcoal burner's hut.

In the evening Booni came home. He was glad to

29

see the strangers, for he never had guests from the out-side world. Sarah served supper and, afterwards, the three men went outside. They sat down on the wooden bench and lit their pipes. Blumkeh and her mother stayed in the hut.

The charcoal burner and the merchant talked quietly, puffing at their pipes. But the young man paid no atten-tion to them. He couldn't forget pretty Blumkeh and kept glancing toward the hut. And from within, through the small, square window, a pair of bright blue eyes watched him in the moonlight.

With the first rays of the sun, the two merchants and Booni went back to the wagon. The charcoal burner helped them make a new axle. Then the father and son hitched up their horses and left. The horses trotted along briskly. But Sholem's head was bowed and his eyes were half closed. His father looked at him and said: "Are you still brooding over that axle? Forget it!"

His son didn't answer. The merchant shrugged his shoulders.

When they came home, Sholem's mother saw that her son was not happy—a mother's heart senses things—and she questioned him.

"Mother, I met a girl in the woods," her son told her. "She is as beautiful as the seven suns in the seven heavens. I can't forget her."

30

"Oh, Sholem! You've been bewitched by a fairy in the woods!" exclaimed his frightened mother.

"No, no!" Sholem assured her. "It was a real girl— the daughter of a charcoal burner." Then he told her all about it.

His mother went to his father and said: "You must go back to the woods and find this girl. Perhaps she has fallen in love with our son. Perhaps their marriage was ordained in heaven, and it was not by chance that the axle broke so near the charcoal burner's hut."

So early the next morning, the merchant hitched his horses to the wagon and went back to the woods. He took both his wife and his son along with him. When they came to the hut in the woods, the merchant said to Booni: "My son, Sholem, can't forget your daughter, Blumkeh."

"Strange," answered Booni, "my daughter, too, has been pining and longing for your son."

"Then all is well," said the merchant. "Let them be married at once."

"Fine!" said Booni. "But, first let me go into town. I'll buy a white gown for Blumkeh, and some good wine, too. I'll bring back a fine cake and stuffed fish. We shall have a wedding that befits a man of your station."

"I don't want to wait till you came back from the city," interrupted Sholem impatiently. "There is no need for wedding gowns, for fine cakes or wine. I want to be married now."

"If it doesn't make any difference to you," said Booni, "then I don't mind either. But we *must* have a witness to the wedding and nobody lives in these woods but us."

"Well, then," said the merchant, "I'll go back to the road and, if someone comes by, I'll bring him here as a witness." And he left at once.

Then Booni told his wife to prepare the wedding meal and turning to Blumkeh, he said, "I have a little wine here on the shelf. Bake some cakes to go with it."

"But I can't bake any fine, tasty cakes," protested Blumkeh. "I can only make plain cornmeal cookies."

"Well, make whatever you can," said her father. "Your mother's busy enough."

Meanwhile the merchant stood in the road and waited.

Late in the afternoon, he saw a hunched-over, tattered beggar with an unkempt beard approaching.

The merchant thought to himself: "He doesn't look like much—but if one hasn't white bread for the Sabbath, black bread will do. If there's no stuffed fish, a herring's food, too."

So the merchant said to the beggar: "Would you come with me to a hut in the woods? We need a witness to a wedding. There'll be wine and something to eat, too."

When Simple Shmerel heard "something to eat," he followed the merchant eagerly. Once at the hut, the ceremony was performed. Then Sarah took the wine from the shelf and served it with the corn cakes that Blumkeh had made. The bridegroom took a cooky, bit into it, and made a wry face. His father and mother took some cookies, too, but after the first taste they both politely put them down. The cookies were so plain and so dry! But Simple Shmerel was just delighted with them and smacked his lips over every one he ate.

When the others saw how much the beggar enjoyed the cakes, they gave him more—and then still more. Simple Shmerel took all they gave him. He ate as many as he could and put the rest in his sack. He didn't have such fine food every day.

The next morning, Sholem took his young wife to his father's grand house in the big city. Blumkeh became a favorite at once. "She is as beautiful as the seven suns in the seven heavens," everyone said. And Sholem was so proud of his lovely bride that he showered precious gifts upon her and devoted himself only to making her happy.

But praise went to Blumkeh's head. When she looked about her at the finely carved furniture and the thick, soft rugs, she thought that everything had been made just for her. And since there was nothing she had to do, she

33

idled her time away all day, thinking only of little ways to please herself.

One morning when she awoke the room was flooded with the light of the sun. "What a lovely day," thought Blumkeh. "I must go down into the garden at once." So, tossing her silken blankets aside, she sat up in bed, lowered her feet to the floor, and searched about with her toes for her slippers. But, unluckily, they weren't in place. She bent down and looked for them impatiently. No slippers! Such carelessness!

"Where are my slippers?" she shouted angrily. "What happened to them?"

Her maids ran into the bedroom and asked fearfully, "What is the matter, mistress?"

"Lumps of flesh! Where are my slippers?

The maids hurried out and brought back a pair of slippers. Blumkeh took one look at them and grew more excited than ever.

"What kind of slippers are these? I want the silk ones trimmed with fur. My feet can't stand this *hard leather!*"

"We thought," answered one of the maids timidly, "that the mistress is fond of these red leather slippers."

"I'll teach you not to talk back to me!" Blumkeh screamed, throwing the leather slippers at the girl.

The maids ran off and Blumkeh wept with rage.

Sholem brought her the slippers of silk and comforted

her. He spoke softly, and wiped the tears from the pretty cheeks with a silken kerchief. Blumkeh sobbed as if in agony. This vexed her husband. Just yesterday she'd been running about barefoot, dressed in a cheap cotton dress and now—

But he didn't say anything to her.

Blumkeh grew worse from day to day. She was cruel to her maids and insulting to her mother-in-law. Her young husband watched unhappily. He tried to change her with soft words; then with harsh words; but nothing helped.

One Friday night, Sholem came from the synagogue with a beggar as his guest for the Sabbath. They honored the poor man and treated him kindly, making room for him at the table with the others. But not Blumkeh! She wrinkled her little nose with disgust at the very thought of sitting near him.

Her husband begged her not to violate the holiness of the Sabbath—not to shame a poor stranger. Reluctantly she remained at the table. But she didn't stay long. When the stranger finished eating his stuffed fish, he wiped his mouth with the back of his hand. At that Blumkeh jumped up and shouted angrily, "I won't sit at the same table with him! Either he goes to the kitchen or I leave the table!" And she ran from the dining-room, rushed to her own room, and locked herself in.

35

When her husband saw how she was carrying on, he thought: "Riches are not good for Blumkeh. Wealth has spoiled her. There's just one thing to do. I must threaten to divorce her. Maybe she'll come to her senses, remember her poor hut in the woods, and be sorry. Then, a divorce won't be necessary."

He brought her before the Rabbi and unloaded his heavy heart. The Rabbi listened to Sholem's story, and then said, "You seem to be justified in your complaints, but I must first hear your wife's story."

But Blumkeh, angry and offended, shouted, "If he wants a divorce, let him have it! I'm through with him!"

The Rabbi looked at the young couple, and saw that though they were excited and angry, now and then, one would steal a longing glance at the other. So he said, "Won't you change your minds, children?"

But Blumkeh answered stubbornly, "No! He wants a divorce—let him have it!"

"Let it be so," added the young man wearily.

So the Rabbi told the scribe to write out a divorce. The old scribe hesitatingly selected a square piece of parchment. He picked out a blunt quill and sharpened it. He sat down at the table and began to write—slowly, laboriously, as though his fingers were unwilling to write the unhappy words. All was still in the room, except for the scratching of the quill on the parchment.

36

Then, through an open window came the sing-song of
a beggar,

Good people, kind people, have pity on me!
Listen to a starving beggar's plea:
Alms, alms, a penny, a crust of bread—
"Feed the hungry," the Lord has said.

"Bring in the beggar," said the Rabbi to the beadle.
"We need a witness to the divorce."

The beadle soon came back with—Simple Shmerel.

The sullen couple took one look and recognized him
at once. It was the very same beggar who had witnessed
their wedding! They both began to feel sorry for what
they were doing, but both were stubborn and didn't say
anything.

Shmerel looked at the couple for a long time, and slowly
he, too, recognized them. Then he remembered the good,
hard cookies. Such cookies! He could still remember
their delicious taste. Maybe they would serve some more
of them. So he turned to the Rabbi and asked, "Will
there be any cookies?"

The Rabbi didn't understand what Shmerel meant.
"A queer fellow!" he thought. "Perhaps I didn't hear
him aright."

"Cookies?" the Rabbi repeated.

"Yes, Rabbi," said Simple Shmerel. "Cookies! How

37

she can bake them! Dry and crisp—they just melt in your mouth!"

Of course, the Rabbi still couldn't understand what the beggar meant, but he saw that the two young people had suddenly turned red and that they were both smiling broadly. The young man was remembering how impatient he'd been to get married, and how he'd even been unwilling to wait until a real wedding meal could be pre-

38

pared, so much had he been in love with Blumkeh. The young wife was thinking of how poor she'd been before her marriage and how she couldn't even bake a proper wedding cake. So they both lowered their eyes, their hearts full of regret.

The Rabbi noticed this and said, "Well, children, do you still want the divorce?"

Neither answered him. He took this as a good sign and said to the scribe, "Tear up the divorce!"

The old scribe was so pleased he obeyed eagerly.

"And now," said the Rabbi to the young man, "we'll serve wine and cookies!"

Simple Shmerel stuffed his mouth with cake and rejoiced.

Sholem, too, munched a cookie happily and said, "You were right, stranger. They were good cakes!" Then he smiled to Blumkeh whose bright blue eyes laughed back at him.

Shmerel ate as much as he could and stored the rest away in his sack. After the celebration, the young man wished to reward him. But Simple Shmerel refused to take any money. "I have enough," he said, "I have enough."

Then Simple Shmerel left the house and disappeared into the great, wide world.

39

Cruel Yigdal

FAR AWAY, IN A GREAT CITY, THERE LIVED a very rich man by the name of Yigdal. He owned great stretches of field and miles of forest. Villages and towns belonged to him. His factories were scattered through many lands; his huge granaries could be seen in every port. His ships sailed the seven seas—ships loaded with ivory and spices from India, fruits and dyes from the Near East, silks and furs from China, pearls from faraway islands in the Pacific and uncut diamonds from Africa.

This rich man, Yigdal, lived in a great palace tended by hundreds of servants. The palace was surrounded by beautiful gardens. In the gardens, there were little streams and pretty lakes in which shining goldfish played and swam. Nightingales nested in the shady trees surrounding the lakes and sang sweetly all night long. Among the trees grew bright yellow daffodils, deep red roses, and snow-white lilies.

Yigdal was not only rich, but he was also tall and handsome. His skin was white and fair, his hair ebony black and his eyes deep blue. His dark, pointed beard was silken and glossy. When he put on his rich clothes of brown velvet, trimmed with hammered gold, he looked as impressive as a young prince, and mothers would often wish: "May our sons grow up to be as handsome and wealthy as Yigdal!"

But Yigdal was like a beautiful red apple that nourishes a worm within itself. For the handsome Yigdal had an evil heart—a black and evil heart. He treated his laborers like slaves and his servants like dogs. There wasn't an ounce of kindness or pity in the man.

Everyone in the city knew of Yigdal's cruelty and no one ever came to him for help. But sometimes it happened that a wandering beggar, who did not know of Yigdal's evil ways, would come to him for alms. Yigdal would listen quietly and say:

"So you want some money, eh? Well, open my safe and help yourself!"

"What do you mean—" the beggar would stammer. "Open your safe? But—I—don't—understand—"

Then Yigdal would lead the bewildered beggar to the big fireproof safe which was always kept locked, bang his fist on the heavy, massive steel doors and mockingly cry:

"Open it and take as much as you want! I have locked my gold and silver and jewels in this strong steel safe that it might be ready for you, and the other good-for-

41

nothings like you, whenever you might have need of it!
But it's safely locked, thank God! Only *I* can open it,
only *I* . . . and *I* *won't!*"

And the poor, frightened beggar would run away as
hungry as he came.

Then there came a hard winter, a winter of heavy
snows, bitter frosts and storms, a winter the like of which
was not remembered by any man. The snows were deep
and the roads poor. It was difficult to bring food into
the town from the surrounding villages, and prices rose.
The poor couldn't pay the high prices. Many of them
roamed through the city, hungry, half-frozen, searching
for food. Many others became sick because they didn't
have enough to eat and couldn't buy wood to heat their
homes. The city was full of misery.

At last all the important citizens, led by the Rabbi, met
to see what could be done to relieve the distress of the
poor. Each one gave as much money as he could, and
many gave more than they could, but still there wasn't
enough.

"Let us go to Yigdal," said one. "Perhaps in times such
as these his heart will take pity on all these poor."

"Don't be foolish," the others answered. "No one can
open *that* safe."

"We must swallow our pride when misery and want are

42

everywhere," said the Rabbi. "Let us see what we can do with him."

So, the next day they called upon the wealthy Yigdal.

They found him sitting on a soft sofa. Beside him, on a little table, were meats, rich cakes and bottles of old wine. The room was warm and bright. Yigdal wore a gown of gold brocade and reclined on soft cushions. He was sipping his wine and munching cake.

The Rabbi looked at the polished floors covered with soft rugs, at the walls hung with tapestries, and said:

"Yigdal, you are a man blessed in all things. You have everything a mind could think of and all a heart could wish for. But in the city the people are cold and hungry. Won't you help your fellow men?"

Yigdal took a walnut from the plate, cracked it with a silver nut-cracker, put the kernel in his mouth, chewed it slowly, took a sip of wine, and grinned:

"Open the safe and help yourself."

"Don't mock us!" said the Rabbi angrily. "This is no time for jesting. People are starving. You, too, may some day be hungry. Don't be so sure that you are forever safe from want and misfortune."

"Of course I am," answered Yigdal, haughtily. "My fields are rich and fertile; my granaries are filled with corn and wheat and all kinds of grain; my mills are grinding my flour; my forests are growing; my factories

are busy; my ships carry my wares to all the corners of the world. What have I to fear? Should there be a drought, I still have my granaries. Should my granaries be destroyed, I have my factories. Should my factories and forests burn, I still have ships scattered over the seven seas. And if my ships should sink, I have gold and silver and jewels in my safe."

"And what will you do, Yigdal, if all these starving and suffering people turn upon you in their misery, break into your mills, your factories, your granaries, even your palace, and rob you of all your riches?"

"I have well-trained soldiers who will shoot down the beggars like dogs. And if the worst comes to the worst, I have swift Arabian horses in my stables to carry me far across the border. I have plenty of money stored away in foreign lands."

The Rabbi nodded his head with pity.

"Yigdal, it seems that you were born with an evil heart," he said. "You do not know the joy of giving. Outside the walls of your palace there are starving people, and here you warm yourself by the glow of your useless gold. But remember what I have told you: no one is sure of tomorrow, no one is safe forever from pain and misery and hunger. There may come a day when even you will starve in your own palace, among all your riches."

Yigdal laughed aloud.

Spring came, and then summer. Food became more plentiful and the troubles of the terrible winter were forgotten. But the townspeople remembered Yigdal with loathing. Yigdal didn't care.

One beautiful mid-summer morning, Yigdal finished his breakfast and went for a stroll in his cool and shady gardens. Then he came back to the palace and sat down at his great oak desk to take care of some business. After he finished his work, he remembered that it had been a long time since he had looked over the treasures in his safe.

Yigdal's safe was very large—a room in itself. He opened the massive steel doors, went in and began to count his money. This kept him busy a long time. When he was through, he was tired, but content. He had more gold, more silver than ever before. He turned to leave, and to his horror found that the great steel doors had accidentally closed behind him. He knew that he was trapped. The doors could not be opened from within the safe, even though they were not locked. They could only be opened from the outside.

Still he pushed fiercely at the heavy doors. He might as well have tried to move a mountain. He banged on the doors with his fists. He shouted and screamed. He hurled the heavy iron drawers full of gold and jewels against the sides of the safe. Someone would surely hear him, he hoped. But no one heard him and no one opened the safe.

After a while Yigdal sat down on the floor and thought. He thought and schemed for hours, but to no avail. He became hungry. He began to scream again and to pound the doors, until at last, exhausted, he fell asleep. He slept until hunger woke him. Then he started pacing up and down the vault trying to think of a way out. Desperate, he screamed with rage and hurled bags of gold to the

46

floor. He looked at the gold pieces flowing from the ripped bags and wept bitterly.

Six days and six nights passed. Lying, almost in a stupor, on the cold stone floor of the vault, Yigdal remembered the Rabbi's words: "No one is sure of tomorrow— safe forever from misery and want. There may come a day when even you will starve among all your riches."

"The Rabbi was right," Yigdal murmured and fell into a faint.

Simple Shmerel wandered from village to village, from town to town and from city to city, a tattered beggar, no different from any other beggar on the road. He went from house to house, begging for alms and singing his ditty:

> *Good people, kind people, have pity on me!*
> *Listen to a starving beggar's plea:*
> *Alms, alms, a penny, a crust of bread—*
> *"Feed the hungry," the Lord has said.*

One day, Shmerel came to the city where Yigdal lived. Some idlers caught sight of the tattered beggar and winked at one another. "Hello, stranger!" they said to Simple Shmerel. "Do you want to get a good meal—

47

and some money besides? Go to Yigdal's palace. There they welcome beggars with open arms—and closed fists," they added, under their breaths.

"And where is this good man's palace?" asked Shmerel eagerly.

The jokers slapped each other on the back and laughed. "He is as sharp as the blunt edge of an axe!"

They showed him the way to Yigdal's palace.

Simple Shmerel came to the palace and, standing outside the huge gates, chanted his song. The servants heard him and laughed. "Here's where we have some fun!" They were in a good humor, these servants. Yigdal had suddenly disappeared and hadn't left anyone in charge of the palace. He had even forgotten to lock the wine cellar. The servants were having a good time for once.

"Do you want alms, stranger?" they taunted Simple Shmerel. "Good. We'll give you all you want. Just open the safe and help yourself!"

"Where is this wonderful safe?" asked Simple Shmerel.

"He is even simpler than he looks," whispered the servants. "Just let him try to open the safe! It'll be something to see."

"The safe?" they said, winking to each other. "We'll show you the way."

They led Shmerel through the long hallways to the massive steel safe.

48

"Just open it and help yourself," they said, pointing to the closed doors.

Simple Shmerel did just as he was told. He went up to the safe and turned the handle. To the amazement of the servants, the heavy steel doors opened, and there lay Yigdal in a faint.

It took Yigdal many months to recover. But from that day he was a changed man. He gave up his evil ways and devoted all the rest of his life to helping the poor and the needy.

Simple Shmerel stayed with Yigdal for a long time. Then, when the wandering beggar was ready to leave, Yigdal loaded him with gifts of gold and jewels. Simple Shmerel stuffed them all into his beggar's sack, went out of the palace, and once again disappeared into the great, wide world.

49

The Wanderer's Return

SHOLEM SHEPSIL WAS A LITTLE MAN, yet he had three fine humps: a very big one on his back, a fairly big one on his chest, and a tiny one on the tip of his nose. Why should one man, and such a little man at that, have three such fine humps? Many a curious child would ask Sholem Shepsil that question. And this was the story he would tell the children:

It happened when the Lord God created man. After He had made Sholem Shepsil, He looked at him and sighed contentedly, "How beautiful he is! Here," He said to the angels, "use him as your model, and form other men in his likeness."

The angels put Sholem Shepsil on a platform and began modeling other men like him. Sholem Shepsil watched them. He saw them taking clay from many different heaps—clay for hands, clay for feet, clay for noses and clay for fingers. So Shepsil thought: "If I had some of that clay, I too would create a man—a little man as tiny as a doll who would talk, eat and walk about, just like a human being."

50

After the angels finished their day's work, they said to Sholem Shepsil, "You may go now." Sholem went down from the platform, stealthily took bits of clay from each heap, and rolled them all into a tiny ball. As Sholem Shepsil walked calmly away, a Supervising Angel noticed that he was holding something in his fist.

"Hey you, over there!" shouted the Angel. "What are you hiding in your hand?"

Sholem Shepsil pretended not to hear the Angel. The Supervising Angel became angry. He took a huge lump of clay and, throwing it at Shepsil's back, hit him right between the shoulder-blades.

"I mean you!" shouted the Angel again.

Sholem Shepsil, bent over from the weight of the lump on his back, turned around and faced the Angel.

"Why did you hit me, Lord Angel?" he asked innocently.

"Just one day old and you're trying to be smart!" jeered the Angel. "Come here and let me sce what you're hiding there!"

Sholem Shepsil saw that he was caught red-handed. He made believe that he was wiping his forehead and stuck the little lump of clay on the tip of his nose. The Angel saw that Sholem Shepsil's handsome nose had suddenly gotten a bump, and laughed. He took another lump of

51

clay and threw it at Shepsil, catching him right on the chest.

"Here's another present, clever one!" he said, laughing. "On your way now!"

And Sholem Shepsil would always end his story with:

> And so these three lumps of clay
> Have stuck to me till this very day.

"Is it really true?" the children would ask eagerly.

"It's true, as all stories are true." Sholem Shepsil would answer solemnly.

"Tell us another," the children who flocked to his orchard would beg.

Sholem Shepsil would make himself comfortable on a bench under an apple tree, bite into an apple, and begin another story:

"Three years ago, early in the spring, right after the apple blossoms fell from this tree, I noticed that one green apple seemed different from all the others. I watched it. Children, I saw that apple grow bigger and bigger day by day. I could almost see it grow right before my eyes. Then, one day, the twig that held the apple began to bend. Fearing that the twig would break, I propped it up with a stout, thick stick. A few days later I saw that the twig was safe but that the branch that held

52

the twig was beginning to sag. I supported the branch with the trunk of a young fir tree.

"In two weeks the apple grew so big that it pulled the whole apple tree to one side. Now I could do nothing. I could only pray that the trunk of the tree would not snap. So I waited and watched, I watched and waited. How much bigger would that apple grow? And the apple grew and grew, and then it was so big that, though it hung from the highest branch of the tree, it almost touched the ground. I spread a blanket on the earth to keep the apple from rotting and hoped that it would come to rest before the tree snapped. All that night, I stayed awake, watching it anxiously. Then, at last, the very next morning, it touched ground and all was well.

"But the apple kept on growing and growing and growing. In time it began to turn red, and when it was ripe at last, it was much bigger than its tree. I borrowed two ladders, tied them end to end, and climbed to the top of the apple. It took me two whole weeks to cut up the apple. My cellar and my garret were filled with barrels of apple, and the cider that I made from that apple has lasted to this very day."

And Sholem Shepsil would point to a corner of his orchard and end *this* story with: "There, underneath that bent apple tree, you can see the very spot where my apple rested on the blanket. The ground became hard as rock from the weight of it and you can see for yourself that nothing will ever grow there again."

There was always a little child who had never heard the story before, and he would ask, awed: "Is it really true, Sholem Shepsil?"

"Of course it's true! Of course it's true!" shouted the older children. "And haven't you heard the rest?"

> *The cow jumped over the moon*
> *And went to the south*
> *Where it burned its mouth*
> *By eating snow with a spoon!*

Sholem Shepsil laughed and then said: "So you don't believe me! Then let's see how smart you are. Say this after me:

> *Kolpak podkolpakom*
> *Kolpakom podkolpak*
> *Kolpak podkolpakom*
> *Kolpakom podkolpak!*"

The children listened fascinated as Sholem Shepsil rattled off the words and tried to repeat them after him. "Kolpak gopadom ... Palkopam ..." they would stutter.

Sholem Shepsil laughed loud and long and then said: "Allright then—here's something easier. Say it after me as quickly as you can.

> *I could if I could,*
> *If I couldn't, how could I?*
> *I couldn't, unless I could,*
> *Could I?*
> *Could you unless you could,*
> *Could ye?*
> *Could ye? Could ye?*
> *Could you, unless you could?*
> *Could ye?"*

All the children clapped their hands, danced around Sholem, and sang in chorus: "No, we couldn't, we couldn't."

"Now that'll teach you that everything I say is true!"

55

said Sholem Shepsil. "It's true, of course it's true. Just as true as—

> *Two deaf men went a mile to hear*
> *A dumb man make a speech;*
> *A blind man watched a cripple climb*
> *A pole to get a peach!"*

Not only was Sholem Shepsil a favorite with all the children, but he was loved by the whole town. Everybody knew him. He was called "Sholem Shepsil, the truth-teller." And whenever anyone would exaggerate a bit or tell a tall story, the people would laugh and say: "Sholem Shepsil's told us *that* already!"

At the end of one fine summer, Sholem Shepsil took a wagonload of his apples to the city to sell. When he came back, he was all excited.

"Have you ever heard the like of it? Simple Shmerel —*our* Simple Shmerel—you remember what the children used to sing about him:

> *Simple Shmerel,*
> *Tall and thin,*
> *Head's a pumpkin,*
> *Brain's a pin!*

Well, just imagine! He's now a great man! When the Prince's treasure-house was robbed, do you know who caught the thieves? Simple Shmerel! A swindler tried to ruin a great merchant, and who do you think discovered it? Pumpkin-head Shmerel! And do you know who saved the life of the great Yigdal? *Our* Simple Shmerel. And all because of his great wisdom and learning."

The townspeople laughed. "Ha! Ha! Ha! This one is the best story yet, Sholem Shepsil!"

Sholem Shepsil was hurt. Usually when people laughed at him, he would laugh with them, but this time he became insulted, and swore that this story was true. The angrier he became, the more the people laughed. "What's become of our Sholem Shepsil? Now he wants us to believe him!"

One day, Sholem Shepsil was standing in the market-place surrounded by the town idlers to whom he was repeating for the hundredth time his story about Shmerel. Still, no one believed a word of it. Suddenly a beautiful carriage drawn by three horses with jingling silver bells rolled into the market-place. Sholem Shepsil took one look at the richly dressed stranger lolling inside the carriage and shouted, joyously:

"Look, it's our *own* Simple Shmerel!"

And so it was. Simple Shmerel had come home.

He gave a great feast in honor of his father and mother. Waiters in dazzling white uniforms served the guests with stuffed fish and fine meats, white bread, honey cakes and strudel, wine and whiskey. Sholem Shepsil drank more than anyone else, ate more than anyone else, and, as usual, talked more than anyone else. Then, at the end of the meal, everybody sang together:

The cow jumped over the moon
And went to the south
Where it burned its mouth
By eating snow with a spoon!

Then they all clapped their hands, turned to Simple Shmerel and cried:

"It *is* true, it *is* true!"

Everyone expected Simple Shmerel to settle down and live the rest of his years in the little village. And so did Simple Shmerel, but ...

59

The Boastful Duke

OW WHEN SHMEREL CAME BACK rich and famous, his fellow townsmen were puzzled. They didn't know how to treat him. Should they respect him, as the outside world did, or laugh at the rest of the world, because *they* knew better? When the people would meet him in the street and see how neatly he was dressed, how dignified he looked, they would greet him politely. Later, they would wonder at themselves. Imagine saying "good-morning" to Pumpkinhead!

Shmerel tried hard to make friends with his neighbors, but he couldn't. He could never say the things that he wanted to say. Talking did not come easily to him. After a while the townspeople began gossiping about him behind his back, and soon they were all laughing openly at him. This happened because Shmerel couldn't read Hebrew properly.

When Simple Shmerel would go to synagogue, he would pull his prayer-shawl over his head, take a Hebrew prayer-book, and pray to himself. Slowly he would spell out the holy prayers, swaying backwards and forwards. He was always careful not to read aloud, because he knew that he couldn't pronounce the words correctly. But one day he became so moved by his prayers that he swayed faster and faster, raised his hands to heaven, and suddenly began to pray aloud. The people heard him, stopped their praying, winked at one another, and laughed. "Listen to Pumpkin-head sawing wood!" they said.

Shmerel heard their laughter and stopped in shame, pulling the prayer-shawl over his face.

That was the beginning. After a while, the townspeople would laugh and jeer at him at the slightest opportunity.

Simple Shmerel went to the Rabbi and stammered, sorrowfully: "Rabbi, why do they laugh at me?"

The Rabbi looked at Shmerel and thought: "A poor soul in pain."

"Don't go to the synagogue any more," the Rabbi advised Shmerel. "Pray at home—alone."

From that day on, Simple Shmerel never went to the synagogue. On nice days he would put on his prayer-shawl and his phylacteries, and go into the woods near his house to pray. He would stop near a tree, open the prayer-book, and keeping the place with his finger, he would loudly spell out the words. After he had finished, he would always add a prayer of his own.

"O God, Almighty Father, why can't I be like other people? Why don't I talk more? Why don't I laugh more, like the others? Why, O God, Almighty Father?"

In a great castle, near the town, lived a rich and mighty Duke by the name of Horwath. He would spend his winters in the capital, at the court of the King, but every summer he would come to his estate near the town where Shmerel lived.

The mighty Duke was always bragging. More than anything else, he would brag about his horses. True, they were wonderful horses—Arabian stallions, the finest in the land—but the Duke's exaggerations were more wonderful than his horses.

The Duke would often tell of the time he drove his horses beside those of Lord Virshiloff to see whose could run the longer. The Lord's horses ran for two days and two nights, without stopping once, but *his,* Horwath's, ran for four days and four nights. And the only reason that he had stopped them after the fourth day and the fourth night was that *he,* Horwath, had become utterly exhausted for lack of food and sleep. Otherwise, his stallions could have run on and on and on.

But Horwath's proudest boast was that his horses were not afraid of wolves. On the contrary, he claimed, wolves were afraid of his horses. He discovered this, Horwath would tell, one winter night when the servants forgot to lock the stables. His two white Arabian stallions galloped off into the forest. There a pack of starving wolves attacked them. Horwath found his horses the next morning—the two stallions surrounded by thirty dead wolves. The rest of the pack had long since fled. *He,* Horwath, had seen their footprints in the snow with his own eyes! And in his palace were the pelts of twelve of the dead wolves for all who wished to see them. (The reason that he had only twelve pelts, he would say, was that his fierce horses had mangled the other wolves so badly that nothing could be saved of their skins.)

The Duke did not know that everyone in town would laugh at him, saying to one another:

"Where are my horses?"
"In the woods, killing off the wolves."

He never heard of this because in his presence all the townspeople would take off their hats and bow humbly.

But Simple Shmerel heard it many a time. He didn't know what it meant—who ever heard of horses killing wolves? But he liked the sound of . . .

"Where are my horses?
In the woods, killing off the wolves."

One day Simple Shmerel stood at the edge of the forest and prayed. He was so lost in his prayers that he didn't hear the approach of a horseman.

The rider was startled by the strange sight of a man wrapped in a prayer-shawl. "This must be a holy man," he thought. "He has gone into the woods where he can commune with God in solitude."

He reined in his horse and asked: "Holy Man, do you know where my horses are?"

Shmerel was startled by the voice. Automatically, without turning his head, he answered:

"In the woods, killing off the wolves."

The rider spurred his mount and galloped off into the woods.

After a short ride he found his horses, all covered with sweat and foaming at the mouth, huddled together in a clearing, encircled by a pack of wolves. The rider emptied his pistol into the air to frighten away the wolves and took his horses home.

The next day Duke Horwath came into town and asked: "Where does the Holy Man live?"

"Holy Man? What Holy Man?"

"The one who prays in the woods."

The townspeople realized with astonishment that the Duke meant Simple Shmerel. They winked at each other but said nothing.

"Your Highness must mean Simple Shmerel. He lives at the other end of town," piped up Sholem Shepsil from the silent crowd.

"Simple Shmerel!" roared the Duke. "I asked for a Holy Man, not a simpleton!"

"But he *is* a Holy Man, your highness," answered Sholem Shepsil. Then he pushed himself to the front and told the Duke the story of Simple Shmerel's miracles.

After the Duke heard Sholem Shepsil's story, he turned his horse's head and galloped off to Shmerel's house. He found Shmerel outside, mending a window.

The Duke jumped down, bowed low, and said: "Holy Man, you saved my priceless Arabian horses. I have brought you a present as a token of my gratitude."

Simple Shmerel took the gift, but didn't say a word.

66

"Holy Man," continued the Duke, "I have heard of the miracles you have performed. I want you to come to my palace and be my advisor."

Simple Shmerel looked fearfully at the Duke and said nothing.

The Duke wondered at Shmerel's silence, but thinking that he wasn't satisfied with the offer, continued: "Holy Man, I'll build a tower for you. I'll give you servants and riches, everything your heart may desire. Please come, I beg you, Holy Man!"

"I can't," mumbled Simple Shmerel.

The Duke was angry, but he controlled himself and said: "I have need of you. Come to my castle and be my prophet, my miracle-worker."

Simple Shmerel lowered his eyes and mumbled again, "I can't."

"You must!" thundered the Duke, losing patience. "I, Duke Horwath, have spoken. Tomorrow you shall come to my castle. If you will not come, you shall know the anger of Duke Horwath! I will burn your flesh with hot irons and cut off your insolent tongue! All the Jews in the town will suffer for your stubbornness!"

That night Simple Shmerel ran to the Rabbi and stammered fearfully:

"Rabbi, what do they want of me? Everybody is always saying, 'Where are my horses? In the woods, killing off the wolves.' and nothing happens. I say it just once, and look what happened!"

"I know," said the Rabbi. "I have heard."

"What shall I do?" wailed Simple Shmerel.

"Do as the Duke says—for your sake, and for the sake of the Jews of the town."

"But I'm only poor Simple Shmerel. I can't even read the prayers properly. Why should all this happen to me?"

"It is your fate, my son," said the Rabbi. "You must obey. May the God of Israel protect you."

Simple Shmerel did as he was told.

The Duke built a tall tower for Simple Shmerel and surrounded him with riches and luxury. He even gave him a servant named Reshis to wait on him. But though Shmerel had everything his heart desired, he felt like a trapped animal. He knew that at any moment, the Duke might ask for the impossible.

But months passed and nothing happened.

"It didn't turn out so bad after all," thought Simple Shmerel. Yet, in his heart he was weary of all the luxury. He felt restless. One of these days, he thought, he would steal out of the castle and take to the road again. He would wander once more from village to village, from town to town, and from city to city. He would again be Simple Shmerel, the beggar.

But days passed and Shmerel remained in the tower.

68

It was hard to break away. He would promise himself, "Tomorrow, I'll go." Always tomorrow...

Then something happened in the castle. The Duchess lost a ring. It wasn't an ordinary ring. It had been a present from the Queen herself, and the Duchess did not dare show herself at court without it. The Duke came to Simple Shmerel and said curtly:

"A ring, the gift of the Queen, was stolen from the Duchess. I give you three days in which to find it!"

The Duke bowed and left.

That night Shmerel went to the Rabbi and told him his troubles. "What shall I do now?" wailed Shmerel sorrowfully.

"Do what all Jews do when in trouble—fast and pray to God."

"But why should this happen to me?"

"Who knows the ways of God?" said the Rabbi. "Go back to the castle and pray and fast. May the God of Israel protect you."

Simple Shmerel went home and began his fast. The first day went by and nothing happened. The second day passed. That evening, after the sun had set and work was done, the serfs on Horwath's estate gathered together in the stable and gossiped about the lost ring. An old, half-blind peasant with a mouth full of big, yellow teeth leered slyly and said, "I say he'll get him."

The serfs knew very well what he meant, but still they asked, "Who?"

"The Holy Man, he'll find the thief."

"How do you know?" the servant, Reshis, challenged him.

The old, wizened peasant puffed for a while on his smelly pipe, then slowly answered, "Magic never fails."

"What takes him so long?"

"It takes time," the old man replied, knowingly. "But, you'll see, as soon as the Jew touches anything that belongs to the thief, the magic will work."

The third day passed and the last hour approached. Simple Shmerel was sad. He had fasted and prayed for three days and three nights, just as the Rabbi had said, but nothing had happened. So he folded his prayer shawl carefully and put it away. Forlornly, he walked to the well to break his fast with a drink.

The servant Reshis watched Shmerel sharply. Had he discovered the thief, he wondered. And as he watched, the man's face suddenly paled, for he saw Shmerel take *his*—Reshis' own—dipper from the side of the well, fill it with fresh, cool water, murmur a blessing and raise it to his lips.

"I am lost," quivered the frightened Reshis. "Now the magic will work."

Poor, troubled Shmerel, didn't realize that he had not

70

used his own drinking vessel, but the water was good and he did feel refreshed. He sighed, aloud, "There's nothing else for me to do. I must go to the Duke and tell him the truth." Taking Reshis by the arm, for he was reluctant to go alone, he added, "Come with me, Reshis!"

At the touch of Shmerel's hand, the terrified servant fell to his knees, clutched at the hem of Shmerel's coat and cried, "Holy Man, don't tell him. Don't tell him I have the ring. You know I didn't steal it, you know I found it by accident. The Duke is a harsh master. I work hard and never get enough for myself and my family. My wife is sick, my children are half-starved. When I saw the ring lying in the grass, I thought, the Duke has many rings. He'll never miss this little one. So I hid it under a rafter in the barn until I could sell it. O, Holy Man," wailed Reshis, "have mercy on me! You know everything. You know what I have said is true."

"I know," said Simple Shmerel, blankly.

"Here is the ring, Holy Man. Pray, don't tell the Duke!"

"I won't," said Simple Shmerel.

As the sun set, the Duke came to Shmerel.

"Where is the ring?" he asked.

"Here," said Shmerel, handing it to the Duke.

Horwath looked at the ring with amazement and said to Shmerel, "Good! And who stole it?"

"I cannot tell you that."

"I, Duke Horwath, command it!"

"But the ring wasn't stolen."

"Who told you that?"

"He did," answered Shmerel.

"Oh, *He!* Well, since it was your God who told you," exclaimed the Duke. "I will not insist. You shall be rewarded."

The summer passed and the Duke left for the capital. Now Horwath really had something to brag about. In no time at all, the whole court had learned of the wonders the Duke's Holy Man had performed. The great lords and fine ladies of the court would listen indulgently to Horwath's stories and knowingly smile to one another.

This vexed Horwath. He announced that he would bring the Holy Man, himself, to court. Let them see for themselves what wonders he could do!

A messenger from the Duke came to Simple Shmerel.

"Duke Horwath commands you to come to the King's court."

Poor, frightened Shmerel hurried again to the Rabbi.

"Rabbi, I have to go to the King's court," he wailed.

The Rabbi nodded his head sorrowfully.

"What do they want of me, Rabbi?"

"You must trust in God."

"But I am only Simple Shmerel. What can I say to a King?"

The Rabbi thought a while.

"They want you to perform miracles, Shmerel, and you are no magician," said the Rabbi. "But the Duke thinks you have already performed two miracles. You must explain that they were only accidents. However, you can't say such a thing openly. You would be insulting the mighty Duke. So you must explain it by telling them a story. There are wise men at court. They will understand what you are hinting at."

Shmerel scratched his head. "*I* don't understand, Rabbi," he said.

"Just tell them this little tale. When you reach the court, repeat it, word for word."

It took Shmerel many a day to memorize the Rabbi's story. Then he left for the court of the King.

In the meanwhile, the King had called his courtiers together to plan a test that would baffle Horwath's Holy Man. They decided to hide a nightingale in the King's treasure-vault. Surely, even the Holy Man would never suspect that a little bird was concealed there. But before they could lock the doors on the nightingale, it escaped. They caught it, and again put it into the vault. But once more the little bird flew out just as they were shutting

73

the doors. The third time, they succeeded in trapping it. Now they were ready to challenge the seer.

Fifty soldiers escorted Simple Shmerel to the court. Just as soon as he entered the hall, he quickly repeated the Rabbi's tale.

"If it isn't watched carefully, a bird may twice escape from its cage, but it's impossible a third time when the guard is so strong."

The Rabbi meant to show by this that both of Shmerel's miracles had really been accidents, but now he was so closely watched that even an accident could not happen.

The King was dumbfounded. How could anyone outside the court have known about the bird? It was just a few moments before the Holy Man's arrival that they had made up the test! Meanwhile Simple Shmerel thought: "I can go now. I have done what the Rabbi told me to do." And without even a by-your-leave, he walked out of the palace.

Two Simple Words

IMPLE SHMEREL TOOK TO THE ROAD. No one would know him and no one would demand miracles of him. He was just a beggar again. Alone again and free again.

Sometimes he would think of home. He wanted to go back. But he was afraid that the townspeople would receive him in a manner befitting the great Holy Man they thought him to be. He remembered the Duke and the miracles he would ask for. So Shmerel buried his longing for home deep in his heart and wandered on.

Soon the novelty of being alone and free wore off. He became downcast and depressed. He began to pray fervently. But his prayers did not satisfy him. The prayer-book was written in Hebrew, and Simple Shmerel knew but one language—Yiddish. True, he could spell out the Hebrew words and read the prayers, but still he didn't know what they meant.

Then, one day, Shmerel found a strange prayer-book. On the upper part of each page there was the prayer in Hebrew, but on the lower part of the page the same prayer was printed in ordinary, everyday Yiddish. Simple

75

Shmerel would spell out the Yiddish words, read them aloud, and now he could understand the meaning of his prayers!

A great joy filled Shmerel's heart. It was just like talking, he thought. So Shmerel stopped talking to people. He had always been embarrassed by strangers. Now he had a book to talk with. He kept to himself more than ever; he became silent and was always reading. When he had learned to read the Yiddish prayers, he liked to struggle through the difficult Hebrew and compare the two, word for word. Slowly he began to understand even the Hebrew. Then he was truly content.

He wandered about aimlessly, lost in his prayers and his book. He didn't ask for much. He lived on bread and water, and slept on the bare ground. He would often smile happily to himself.

He didn't bother anybody, and nobody bothered him.

Soon Shmerel knew all the prayers in his thin little book by heart. So he scraped and saved, and bought another prayer-book, the thickest, the heaviest book he could find.

The first prayer in the book was a hymn. It began:

"The whole universe is a song of praise to God. In the morning the birds sing, the sun rises like a red fire, the dew is on the grass, and the hearts of all men are filled with joy. All this is in praise to God."

76

Next morning Simple Shmerel woke earlier than usual, even before dawn, and went into the woods. He walked through the forest, staff in hand, reading the hymn. He looked around him.

"It's all just as the book says. The book must know everything," he murmured to himself.

He turned to the next prayer. There on the top line, in Hebrew, were two words that he had never seen before: "*Aineny Yodaya.*" He looked at the bottom of the page, at the Yiddish translation, to see what the two words meant. "I don't know," he read in Yiddish. He was puzzled. He looked again. Yes, "I don't know" was printed there!

He spelled out the two Hebrew words, pointing with his finger at each letter as he sounded it:

"A-i-n-e-n-y Y-o-d-a-y-a
I d-o-n-'-t k-n-o-w."

Simple Shmerel couldn't understand it. The book didn't know! Two short simple words like "*Aineny Yodaya*" and the book didn't know what they meant! Simple Shmerel rolled the two words over his tongue "*Aineny Yodaya, Aineny Yodaya....*"

He searched through the whole book. Maybe the book found out what the words meant later on. He saw the two words repeated many a time, but always, at the bottom, would be written: "I don't know."

77

So he walked and walked, he thought and wondered. At last, he came out of the woods and onto the highway. He was deep in thought. His head was lowered, his eyes looked blankly at the ground, and he mumbled, *"Aineny Yodaya, Aineny Yodaya."* Suddenly he saw something shining in the dust of the road. He bent down and out of curiosity picked up the shiny thing. It was a bright new gold piece. He threw it away impatiently. Money had gotten him into enough trouble.

"Aineny Yodaya, Aineny Yodaya," he continued, still looking down at the road. Suddenly he saw another ducat, but went on as if he hadn't noticed it. After another five paces he saw three more ducats. He looked away. Another three paces—five ducats in a little heap.

"Trouble again!" sighed Simple Shmerel. "What do they want of me now?" No, he thought, no, he would *not* take the money. But there, a yard away, lay five more ducats in a shining heap, and a few steps further, the highway was littered with gold.

Simple Shmerel stopped. It was an omen; he must obey. So he gathered up all the gold and put it in his sack. The gold was very heavy. Bent almost double by its weight, Simple Shmerel hurried on to the nearest city, worried, still wondering. . . .

In the city, an excited crowd had gathered in the

Rabbi's house. An angry man with a red face was shouting furiously and waving his hands with excitement. Near him stood another man, pale and trembling.

"Rabbi!" cried the angry, red-faced man. "Make him give me back my money! Make the thief give back the money he stole from me!"

"Listen to him," interrupted the pale, trembling man, lifting his eyes beseechingly. "I have worked faithfully for him these last twelve years. I have been an honest, loyal servant and these are the thanks I get!"

"Be calm," said the Rabbi. "Tell me what happened."

"Three weeks ago, Rabbi," said the red-faced man, "we went to the Leipzig fair to buy some leather. I took twelve hundred ducats with me. I was afraid to carry so much money, so we pried loose one of the boards of the driver's box and hid the money there. Then I nailed the board down. Only the two of us knew the secret—my trusted servant and I.

"I kept my eye on the box. No sooner would we stop for the night than I would examine the hiding-place. But last night, when we arrived in the city, I didn't bother because it was late and I was tired and sleepy. What a fool I was!

"Early this morning I hurried down to the stables, just to make sure. And what did I see? My trusted servant was standing beside the wagon, pressing the board down

79

so that it should be tight. I pushed him aside and ripped up the board. My twelve hundred ducats were gone! Every one of them—except ten that had fallen into a crack. Rabbi, I caught the thief red-handed, and he can't deny it!"

"He did see me fastening the board," mumbled the

other man, "but I didn't steal any money. I went to the stables to see to the horses and noticed that the board was loose. I fastened it, not even thinking to look inside. I heard a cry and turned around. There he stood, waving his arms and shouting, 'Help, help!' I know it is hard to believe my story, but I swear that I didn't steal anything. Search me! You'll see that I haven't got the gold!"

"Ha! Search him!" screamed his master scornfully. "What good would that do? He isn't fool enough to carry the money with him. He has hidden it somewhere. Make him tell where he's hidden it! If you don't, I'll get the police, Rabbi. You know the penalty for stealing! They will cut off his right hand!"

Before the Rabbi could say anything, the door opened and a tattered beggar pushed through the crowd.

"Are you the Rabbi?" asked the beggar.

"Yes."

Silently, the beggar took his sack from his shoulder and emptied it on the table. The astonished Rabbi looked at the golden ducats heaped upon the table and asked:

"Where did you get all this gold?"

"I found it."

"Where?"

"Scattered over the road."

Everyone quickly realized that these were the mer-

81

chant's ducats. But, in the excitement, the merchant and his servant were soon forgotten. All eyes were on the beggar.

"Who are you?" asked the Rabbi.

"Simple Shmerel."

"You have saved a man's life, my son," said the Rabbi.

Shmerel didn't say anything. He turned to go. The Rabbi stopped him.

"Don't you want your reward?" asked the Rabbi.

"I don't want any money. I don't need it."

"But can't I do anything for you?" persisted the Rabbi.

"Yes, Rabbi."

"What is it?"

"Tell me, Rabbi! What does 'Aineny Yodaya' mean?"

The Rabbi smiled at the simple question.

"I don't know," he answered.

Shmerel sighed sadly. He turned and walked out of the house.

The Wicked Murdim

SIMPLE SHMEREL WANDERED AIM-lessly for seven months and seven days. On the eighth day of the eighth month he came to the land of King Grabol. Now King Grabol was wicked and cruel and greedy; his ministers were as bad as their master, and the worst of the lot was the King's prime minister, Murdim.

There were no Jews in Grabol's kingdom, but in a country nearby lived many Jews whose ancestors had settled there hundreds and hundreds of years before. They were successful traders and had made their country rich and prosperous.

King Grabol was envious of his wealthy neighbors.

"Let us make war against them," said the King to his minister, Murdim.

So they attacked the neighboring kingdom and conquered it. The merciless Grabol killed many of the inhabitants and confiscated most of their lands. But the Jews suffered most, for the cruel King hated them bitterly.

The prime minister, Murdim, was as sly as he was

mean. He knew how great was the King's hatred for the Jews and, wishing to find favor in the eyes of his master, he said, "Let us drive the Jews out of this land which is now ours, and take away their property and possessions."

"We must have some excuse first," said the King.

The evil-hearted Murdim thought for seven days and seven nights. On the eighth day he came before the King and said:

"Let this be proclaimed throughout the land: The Jews are an accursed people, for they do not believe in the true God, and with their presence defile our land. Therefore, the Senate has decreed that these heretics be exiled and their property confiscated. But the King in his great mercy has commanded that a religious debate be held first. The Jews will be defended by their Rabbis and the Senate by the King's prime minister, Murdim.

"The debate will be held before all the people of the city. A platform will be built in the center of the marketplace and a deep pit dug nearby. The Rabbis have the right to ask the prime minister one question. Should he fail to answer correctly, the Jews will be allowed to remain in the land. But if he does answer correctly, the Rabbis will be thrown into the pit and buried alive; all the Jews will be exiled and their property confiscated. The King will be the sole judge!"

King Grabol laughed.

"Very clever, Murdim, very clever! That's the way to fool them. Show that I am merciful and just. Don't worry, I'll be the right kind of a judge!"

When the proclamation was issued, the Jews realized that it was only a pretext to make their exile legal. They said to their leaders:

"Let us leave this land and give up our possessions. Why shed the blood of our Rabbis needlessly?"

"We will not leave the land in which our forefathers lived," answered their leaders, "the land in which we buried our dead and raised our children. We will not leave, unless we are forced to leave. We must have faith in God."

So the Jews prayed and fasted and waited for the fateful day. A deep pit had been dug in the middle of the market-place. Near the pit was a great platform. On the platform sat the King and his ministers. Near the King sat Murdim, smiling wickedly.

"Don't forget!" whispered King Grabol to Murdim. "Answer their question with anything that pops into your head. Remember, *I* am the judge . . ."

On the same platform, in a corner, were the Rabbis, pale with fasting.

On that day Simple Shmerel arrived. Following the crowds to the public square, he suddenly heard the blast

85

of a trumpet. A herald on the platform proclaimed:

"Silence! The debate between the Jews and the chief minister is about to begin. Any Jew may ask any question of the chief minister in any language. Nothing is hidden from the chief minister, Murdim. He is the wisest man in the kingdom of our King Grabol."

Simple Shmerel's eyes became bright.

"Here is the man for whom I've been waiting!" he thought. "He knows everything."

86

Shmerel pushed his way through the crowd, walked right up to the platform, and shouted excitedly:

"What does '*Aineny Yodaya*' mean?"

Murdim smiled to himself. He knew Hebrew very well. It was such an easy question, he thought, that he might as well give the right answer. So, laughing, Murdim promptly shouted back:

"I don't know! I don't know!"

The King grew red with anger. Murdim had betrayed him! He must have been bribed by the Jews. He'd show that smart minister of his that no one could trick King Grabol!

"He doesn't know!" roared the King, furiously waving his sword. "Throw *him* into the pit! Throw him in!"

The startled soldiers immediately obeyed their master.

The Jews shouted for joy and turned to look for their saviour, but Simple Shmerel had already disappeared in the crowd.

"He didn't know, either," he murmured sadly to himself.

The bewildered Shmerel left King Grabol's land, still wondering: why had the herald said that nothing was hidden from the chief minister, Murdim? After all, he didn't know what "*Aineny Yodaya*" meant! And stranger still! Why had the King been so angry? And all those

87

generals in gold-braided uniforms, those senators in silk hats, those bishops in their big red hats! Why did they all look so surprised and angry when they heard the chief minister's answer. And why were all the Jews and the Rabbis in their fur caps—those learned men with their deep, clever eyes—so happy that the chief minister, too, didn't know?

It was too much for Simple Shmerel.

The Mysterious Flask

HE SUMMER PASSED, THE AUTUMN too, and then winter.

And in the spring, just before the festival of Passover, Simple Shmerel came to a great city, in which there lived many Jews. He walked through the city and came to the ghetto. Through an open window, he could hear the voices of children studying. He sat down on a bench outside the house and rested.

He leaned on his thick staff and listened to the voices of the children in the *Cheder*. He could hear them very clearly. They were repeating the *Hagadah* after their teacher:

"The Torah speaks of four sons: *Echod chochom*, righteous one, *echod roshoh*, wicked one, *echod tam*, simple one, *echod aineny yodaya*, and one who was . . ."

The startled Simple Shmerel had strained his ears to catch the translation of *"Aineny Yodaya,"* but had missed the words. So he waited patiently until the children were leaving the school. Then he stopped a child and asked:

"Tell me, little boy, what does '*Aineny Yodaya*' mean?"

"I don't know," promptly answered the boy.

"You've already forgotten it?" asked Shmerel wonderingly. "But I just heard you translating it ..."

The child looked wide-eyed at Shmerel.

"That's what it means, funny man!" he said. " '*Aineny Yodaya*' means 'I don't know'."

Shmerel mumbled blankly to himself: " '*Aineny Yodaya*,' I don't know—so that's what it means...."

He was disgusted. He scolded himself angrily.

"Shmerel, you are a simpleton! The children were right when they used to call you pumpkin-head. You ask the Rabbi a stupid question, he answers you, and you think he's ignorant, you think he doesn't know! Nothing can get into your thick skull!"

Passers-by saw a hunched-over, ragged beggar standing in the middle of the street, waving his arms and scolding aloud. They stopped and watched him.

Shmerel didn't see them. He went on:

"You read books. You shouldn't, stupid! You ask questions. You shouldn't, fool!"

No sooner had he said these words than a dreadful thought came into his head. He had already done it! He had already caused trouble for the Jews. The King on the platform had been angry, he had waved his sword and shouted. Shmerel remembered that there had been many rabbis on the platform. The King would punish the Jews for Shmerel's stupid question!

90

So Simple Shmerel beat his chest with his fists and cried out:

"I am guilty! I am guilty!"

The people moved fearfully away. Simple Shmerel ran off, still shouting wildly.

For three days Simple Shmerel wandered about the great city without food or drink. On Passover eve he stumbled into a synagogue and there, tired and thirsty, he fell asleep behind the brick stove.

When he awoke it was night. The synagogue was dark. Over the ark in which the scrolls of the Law were kept, a small lamp burned—the Eternal Light. The little flame dimly lighted the two lions carved on each side of the ark. The doors of the ark were covered with a thick velvet curtain on which were embroidered the Ten Commandments. The golden threads of the embroidered curtains glistened in the dark. Simple Shmerel looked up at the Ten Commandments shining in the dark and thought: "These are the words of God. Behind that curtain is the ark, and in the ark are the holy scrolls. Inside, hidden between the scrolls, is God."

Shmerel drew closer to the ark. If it had been daytime he would never have dared do such a thing. But now, in the darkness of the night, he climbed the few steps with difficulty, pushed aside the curtain, and slowly opened the doors.

He laid his head among the holy scrolls, leaning upon his hands, and prayed for a long time. He felt better. After he was through he closed the two little doors, drew the heavy curtain back into place, and sighed with relief. "God has forgiven me my sins," he thought. Suddenly, by the dim light of the lamp, he saw blood on his hands. He looked at them with horror and leaned weakly against the ark.

At that moment the doors of the synagogue opened. The old Rabbi had come to study, as was his custom. Simple Shmerel ran to the Rabbi, fell on his knees and cried out:

"Rabbi, oh Rabbi, save me, save me!"

"What is it, my son? Who are you?"

"I am Simple Shmerel. Look at my—"

"Stand up, Shmerel, don't kneel," interrupted the Rabbi. "You are a good man. You have always brought help to your brethren."

"No, Rabbi. I am a sinner, a sinner. God has shown me that! See the blood on my hands!"

"Stop crying, my son," said the Rabbi alarmed, looking at Simple Shmerel's bloody hands. "Tell me what happened!"

When Simple Shmerel had ended his story, the Rabbi said:

"Let me see. You opened the holy ark. You laid

your head among the scrolls and supported yourself with your hands. That is, you braced yourself against the floor of the ark. After you closed the doors, you saw that your hands were smeared with blood. Is that right?"

"Yes, Rabbi."

"Be comforted, my son. God has sent you to save us."

"I don't understand, Rabbi."

"It doesn't matter."

"Has God forgiven me my sins, Rabbi?"

"You didn't sin, Shmerel. You have done a holy deed."

"I don't understand, Rabbi."

"It doesn't matter, my son. A messenger does not have to know the meaning of his message. Go now."

Simple Shmerel slung his sack over his shoulder and left.

The Rabbi hurried to the beadle. He knocked at the door and whispered:

"Baruch, wake up, quickly!"

Now in that city lived a shopkeeper named Grabonik. He hated the Jews because his competitor was a Jew. This Jew was sober and thrifty. His store was clean and well-stocked. He paid his bills on time and his credit was good. On Saturday nights, when Grabonik would drink with his friends, he would always end up shouting drunkenly: "Let's kill all the Jews! They are cursed by God. We mustn't stand for them! Let's kill the Jews, I say!"

Grabonik had adopted an orphan boy named Stephan so that people should think him a virtuous and kindly man. But the truth of the matter was that the orphan earned much more than his keep. He took care of the shop, scrubbed the floor, heated the big brick stove, swept the sidewalk, ran the errands, and even did Grabonik's cooking. But nothing could satisfy Grabonik. He was

94

always finding fault with the child and, whenever he was drunk, he would beat Stephan mercilessly.

It happened that year that Easter and Passover came at the same time. Grabonik worked hard because of the holiday. Late one night, after he had wearily closed his shop, he stopped at a tavern for a few drinks before going to bed. He came home drunk and stretched himself on the sofa.

"Take off my boots, blockhead!" he shouted at Stephan.

The boy rushed to his master, dropped to his knees and began struggling with the heavy, muddy boots. Grabonik became furious, cursed Stephan angrily, and kicked him in the stomach. Stephan fell to the floor, twisting in pain.

"Lazy dog, good-for-nothing, pull off my boots!" yelled Grabonik.

"I can't get up," moaned Stephen.

"You ungrateful pig's snout! I'll teach you to talk back to me! I'll show you who's master here!"

Grabonik staggered to his feet, lifted a heavy stool and brought it down with a crash on Stephan's head. Then, dead drunk, he fell to the floor beside the boy.

Early next morning, Grabonik awoke, stretched himself, yawned, and called out: "Where are you, blockhead? Bring me a pitcher of cold water!"

There was no answer. Grabonik sat up, opened his

mouth to shout once more—and saw Stephan lying beside him. Grabonik flew into a rage. "Still asleep, you lazy dog! I'll teach you!" He ran into the yard, filled a pail at the well, and threw the ice cold water over the boy. Stephan didn't move. Grabonik kicked him angrily. Still the boy didn't move. Grabonik pulled him up by the hair and shook him furiously. The body was cold and stiff. Stephan was dead.

For a moment, Grabonik leaned against the wall, pale and frightened. Then he laughed nervously to himself, looked at the motionless body of the boy and muttered: "Maybe it's all for the best. . . ."

It was the first night of Passover and the Jews had gathered together in the synagogue. They were all in a gay, holiday mood. The cantor was singing *"Halel"* when suddenly the heavy doors of the synagogue were flung open and the captain of the guard with his troop of soldiers marched in. Behind them came the mayor and Grabonik.

The mayor pushed the frightened cantor aside and climbed to the pulpit.

"Jews!" he cried, "you have murdered the Christian boy, Stephan. You murdered him for his blood with which to bake your matzohs. We know that some of his blood was put in a bottle and placed in your holy ark together with the scrolls. Captain of the guard, open the doors of the ark!" he commanded.

Through the open doors of the synagogue the shouting of the mob outside could be heard.

"Death to the Jews! Kill the Jews!"

The frightened congregation huddled together.

Only the Rabbi and the beadle were calm. The Rabbi stepped up to the captain of the guard and said:

"That is foolish. Such an accusation has been proven again and again to be false. The matzohs are made of wheat flour and plain water—nothing else!"

"Open the doors of the ark!" shouted the mayor to the reluctant captain.

The captain obeyed, opened the ark and, one by one, took out the holy scrolls. In a corner he found a bottle filled with a brownish liquid, which he handed to the mayor.

"It's nothing but a bottle of raisin wine which we use for our benedictions," said the Rabbi.

"It looks like blood to me," sneered the mayor.

He opened the bottle and sniffed. He turned with surprise to the captain of the guard.

"It does smell like wine," he said. The captain took the bottle and he, too, sniffed.

"Yes, it does," he answered, handing the bottle back to the mayor.

97

The mayor poured a little of the liquid into his hand and cautiously tasted it with the tip of his tongue.

"It *is* wine!" said the surprised mayor.

But Grabonik insisted, excitedly:

"It *can't* be wine! I know it's blood!"

"How can you be so certain?" asked the mayor.

Grabonik proudly thumped his chest with his fist.

"When I say I know, I *know!*" he roared. "I put it there my—" he stopped suddenly, realizing his mistake.

"What was that? What did you say?" asked the captain suspiciously.

"I mean, er ... that is ..." stuttered Grabonik, "I mean that I saw them put a bottle of blood there."

"When was this?" asked the captain.

"Er ... last night ... I hid myself in the synagogue."

"How did you get into the synagogue?"

"Why ... er, uh. . ."

The captain continued to question Grabonik until the confused shopkeeper had to confess that he, himself, had killed the boy and hidden a bottle of the child's blood in the ark.

The Jews thought it a miracle. God had changed the bottle of blood into raisin wine.

Only the Rabbi and the beadle knew that it was Simple Shmerel who had saved them.

In Those Days

IMPLE SHMEREL LEFT THE CITY. AT last he was comforted. The Rabbi had told him: "You didn't sin, Shmerel." So he was happy again.

He wandered for many years at peace with himself, and always thumbing his books. He never annoyed people with questions; he avoided them as much as he could. Often he would sleep in the open fields or in the woods under a tree.

In the stillness of the night, he would sometimes be awakened by the cry of a lonely bird or the bellow of a wild animal. He would lie awake in the dark, look up at the stars winking at him through the branches, and soon fall asleep again. Then he would dream of animals with eyes bright as stars and beautiful birds shaped like branches. And Shmerel didn't know whether he had dreamed these things or whether he had really seen them.

One night Simple Shmerel came to a great river. He lay down to sleep in a nearby field when suddenly he was awakened by strange noises. From afar, he heard the sound of trumpets, the stamp of horses' hoofs, and the tramping of many feet. Just before dawn, he saw the sky redden as though great fires were burning beyond the horizon. And these things Shmerel knew he had not dreamed.

Simple Shmerel crossed the river and wandered up into the mountains. That evening he was looking for an overhanging ledge or a cave in which to sleep when a man suddenly came from behind a boulder. The stranger was dressed in a heavy sheepskin coat and wore a peasant's cap on his head. His full beard was a fiery red, and there was a brilliant light in his eyes. Despite his simple clothes, he seemed to Shmerel a messenger from God. The man came up to Shmerel and said:

"*Sholem aleichem,* peace be with you! You are Shmerel, are you not?"

Shmerel fell to his knees before this awe-inspiring man and mutely nodded his head. Naturally, he didn't know that the stranger had recognized him from all the stories he had heard about the tattered wanderer.

"Rise up, Shmerel! I am glad you have come. Follow me!" the man said, kindly.

They went on together until they reached a hut. Three of the walls were made of thin boards covered with branches. The fourth wall was the bare side of a cliff. Inside the hut it was warm and clean.

Simple Shmerel noticed that the hut was filled with

manuscripts and books, and he thought: "All alone in the mountains. A hut full of books. Strange!" But he didn't say anything.

The man with the red beard asked Shmerel to eat with him. They ate in silence. After supper, the stranger puffed slowly at a long-stemmed pipe and watched Shmerel closely, but he didn't say a word. A little later they went to bed.

In the middle of the night, Shmerel awoke. He opened his eyes and saw the red-bearded Jew sitting at the window, reading the Gemorah aloud by the light of the moon. Shmerel listened to the sweet sing-song and envied the stranger. If only, he, Shmerel, could be as learned as that! After listening for a long time, Shmerel rose, went up to the man, and tapped him on the shoulder.

"Can you teach me the Gemorah, stranger?" he asked.

The man stopped his reading and looked at Shmerel. "No," he said.

"Why not?"

"It is not your work."

"What *is* my work?"

"You will be told."

"Are you a Rabbi?"

"Not yet. Now I earn my living chopping wood. But later on, I shall be known as the *Baal Shem*—the leader of the Jews."

101

"Is that why you study so much?" asked Shmerel.

"Yes."

"May I stay with you?" asked Shmerel.

"No," answered the stranger. "There is no time to lose. Our people are in danger. Tomorrow, you must go back to the river where you heard the noises of war. The Cossacks have revolted against the Poles and are killing innocent Jews. *You* can stop it."

"How?"

"I don't know yet. Go back to the river. I'll meet you there."

On the way to the river Simple Shmerel saw fields laid waste, huts burned down, and villages in ruin. He reached the river and crossed it.

He wandered for days. Then, he met a band of beggars. Some were blind, some were lame, but they all carried guitars and sang merrily as they went along.

A beggar with a fiery red beard approached Shmerel.

"Where are you going, brother beggar?" asked the red-beard.

"Nowhere," answered Shmerel, curtly.

"Come with us to the city. We are going to the city now," said the beggar with the red beard.

"And what shall we do in the city, in the city?" sang out a blind beggar, strumming on his guitar.

"That's where our brother Cossacks are, that's where our brother Cossacks are," answered a lame beggar.

"And what are they doing, what are they doing?" hummed a third.

"They are shooting the Poles and killing the Jews, killing the Jews," sang a fourth.

"And there we shall have our fun!" chanted the whole band.

Shmerel looked at them, bewildered.

"Come with us," said the beggar with the red beard again.

"I'm not going," answered Shmerel, tearfully.

"I said, come with us!" insisted the beggar.

Simple Shmerel didn't answer, and turned away. The red-bearded beggar strummed on his guitar and hummed:

> "Mountains, a hut,
> A stranger with a red beard . . ."

Simple Shmerel was startled. A familiar voice! A familiar face! A familiar red beard! He looked closer at the beggar.

"I'll go with you," said Shmerel.

For many years, the Polish lords had cruelly oppressed their Cossack subjects. But now the wild Cossacks had rebelled and in their fury, they were wreaking their spite upon the poor, unfortunate Jews who happened to be in the way.

The Poles were afraid to resist because it seemed that the great Russian queen had given her approval to the Cossack Gonta, the leader of the revolt. His army had overrun the city and he had taken the best Jewish house right in the middle of the market-place for his head-quarters. Now he sat at the head of the table surrounded by his staff, drinking corn whiskey and bellowing his commands: "Wipe out the Jews! Kill all the unbelievers! Don't spare the women or children! Not a soul must remain alive! Don't be afraid! The whole Russian army is behind us. The Poles won't dare defy us by protecting the Jews. I have the Golden Gramota—the license. The Russian Queen gave it to me. I have the Golden Gramota!"

The Cossacks pillaged the city, set it afire, and killed all the Jews they could find. They seized what they could carry and destroyed whatever they couldn't. They guzzled corn whiskey, killed and plundered, and roared drunkenly the songs of their native steppes.

Simple Shmerel wandered with the beggars through the city and saw the empty, gutted houses, the streets littered with broken furniture, torn clothes and pillow feathers. Through the broken doors, he saw ripped curtains, smashed tables and the scattered pages of torn books. Many of the houses had been burnt to the ground and only the blackened chimneys remained. From the tents, pitched in the streets, he heard snatches of song, mixed with the drunken laughter of soldiers and the playing of guitars and accordions.

Suddenly there was a shrill scream.

Simple Shmerel groaned.

"Hey you," cried a blind beggar. "Why do you groan like an old woman?"

"It was a child," answered Simple Shmerel, tearfully.

"Leave them to the Cossacks. They'll take care of them!" leered the blind beggar.

Simple Shmerel groaned once more.

"Are you a true believer?" asked the blind beggar, suspiciously.

"Of course he is," interrupted his red-bearded companion. "He is as true a believer as I am."

"Then why doesn't he sing as we do?"

106

"He hasn't had a drop of whiskey all day," answered the red-bearded one. And, turning fiercely to Shmerel, he shouted: "Shut your mouth, old woman, and if you have to open it, put some whiskey in it!"

But, stealthily, he squeezed Shmerel's hand. . . .

The Baal Shem and Simple Shmerel left the band and passed the night alone in the woods. Shmerel buried his head in his beggar's sack and wept without restraint. The Baal Shem stroked Shmerel's head and murmured: "I know, Shmerel, your heart is heavy. But you must be brave, you have work to do. When I first met you, I knew you had come to save our people. So I sent you back toward the river, while I, myself, disguised as a beggar, went ahead to discover what you must do. I learned that your old servant, Reshis, is now the trusted lieutenant of the Cossack chief, Gonta. Reshis is here."

"Reshis?" questioned Shmerel, uncomprehending. "Who is Reshis?"

"He is the servant whose life you saved many years ago when you lived in Horwath's tower. This once wretched serf has now risen high in the world. You must see him."

"How," asked Shmerel.

"Go back to the city alone. God will guide you."

At dawn, the Baal Shem left Simple Shmerel.

107

Shmerel dragged himself slowly along the highway. He passed a curve in the road and didn't hear the horses that were coming up from behind. Six drunken horsemen were trotting along, driving six Jews between them.

The group came quickly around the curve in the road and Simple Shmerel was swept along with them. Suddenly he felt the crack of a whip over his shoulders and heard the cursing of a Cossack:

"You devil's spawn, what are you doing—walking or sleeping? Step lively there!" And crack! went the whip again.

Simple Shmerel had to run as fast as he could to keep up with the horsemen.

Soon the Cossacks stopped to rest. First, they fed their mounts and then they took bottles of corn whiskey from their high boots. They gulped down the whiskey and jeered at their prisoners.

Suddenly one of the drunken Cossacks exclaimed:

"Look! There are seven Jews! How many prisoners did the chief give us?"

"Six," chorused the other Cossacks.

"But we have seven!"

"You're crazy."

The befuddled Cossack scratched his head.

"Maybe I'm crazy, but I count seven. *You* count them, and see what you get."

108

The second Cossack laboriously counted on his fingers, "One, two, three, four, five, six—seven!"

Another Cossack pushed him aside and counted the prisoners. Seven again! Finally all six horsemen counted together. There were seven Jews, no less. The superstitious Cossacks crossed themselves.

"We are bewitched!" they said fearfully to each other. "Let us hurry back to the chief."

They turned back to the city and brought the seven Jews before their general. When he heard their story, he flew into a rage. "You brainless mules!" he shouted. "You pigs! You're drunk! So drunk you can't count right!"

The Cossacks nodded sheepishly. "True, batko, true, chief, we did take a little nip of whiskey, but we counted right. There are seven Jews here, seven, by God!"

"You dogs! How can there be seven when I gave you six?"

"We were bewitched, and the six Jews became seven..."

"I'll bewitch you—with a horse-whip! When I say there are six, there are six! I'll show you how to count, you ignorant peasants! How many of you are there?"

"We are six," the Cossacks answered.

"All right then. Each of you grab a Jew. We'll see whether there's one left over!"

109

The men obeyed their batko. Each Cossack grabbed a Jew by the scruff of his neck. One Jew remained—a seventh.

The chief looked at the seventh Jew, dropped heavily into a chair, and shouted:

"Whiskey!"

An aide hurried in with a bottle of whiskey. The batko pulled out the cork with his teeth and drained the bottle in one gulp. Wiping his mouth with his hand, he said, "Now my brain is clear. We'll find out which one doesn't belong. Call in the scribe and let him read the names of those whom I gave you to take to the fort."

The scribe called out the names of the six prisoners. Shmerel's name was not on the list.

"Aha!" exclaimed the chief. "So this is the trouble-maker! Who are you, seventh Jew? A magician, eh? We'll see how good your magic is! We'll see whether it'll stop cold steel!"

And unsheathing his sharp sword, the Cossack batko strode toward Shmerel. But when he took one look at the beggar, he paled and stopped short.

"Is it you, Holy Man?" he cried, his unsheathed sword trembling in his hand.

"Yes, Reshis," answered Shmerel.

"What are you doing here?"

"He commanded me to come."

"He?" repeated Reshis, fearfully.

"He," answered Shmerel.

"Look, don't try to frighten me. I'm not afraid of your Jewish God. He can't stop us. We burned His synagogues, we destroyed His Holy Scrolls, we tortured his people. And He could not do a thing!"

Simple Shmerel stood motionless and said nothing. Only his eyes filled with tears.

Reshis was startled and frightened. He had expected the Holy Man to threaten him, to rave at him. But the man whom he feared above all others just stood there, silent. Reshis trembled. The Holy Man still must have some hidden power. So, frenziedly, he pulled out an important-looking document from his pocket, waved it wildly in front of Shmerel, and roared:

"Here! This is the Golden Gramota, the written permission from the Queen. Even your God is powerless before this!"

Seeing the paper brandished so vigorously under his nose, Shmerel put out his hand to take it. Reshis, fearing that the Holy Man might examine the document, whipped his arm back, whereupon the beribboned Gramota flew out of his hand, fell into the roaring fire and was consumed before anyone knew what had happened.

Reshis, paralyzed with fright, fell to his knees and clutched at Shmerel's hands. "So you knew it was forged,

Holy Man. Have mercy on me," he cried. "It wasn't my fault, it was Gonta who did it. He knew that the Poles wouldn't dare protect the Jews if they thought the great Russian Queen was supporting him. Have mercy on me. If you spare my life, I'll go to the Polish generals with you and confess everything."

But Shmerel was so overwhelmed that he did not know what to say. Reshis, completely terrified by Shmerel's ominous silence, felt that he was doomed. Deciding to make one last effort to save his life, he jumped up and shrieked hoarsely:

"We'll go right now. I'll even make them come with us as witnesses," he added, pointing to his Cossack soldiers who had stood by, petrified, throughout this extraordinary scene.

When the Polish generals learned that the Gramota had been forged, they took courage and ordered a surprise attack on Gonta. The Cossacks were defeated. Reshis fell on the battle-field, and Gonta was captured and hanged.

The Jews rejoiced at their deliverance, but once again a poor, tattered beggar set out on his endless wanderings.

His Last Miracle

IMPLE SHMEREL WANDERED AND wandered until he came to a faraway land. It was winter. The sky was a frosty blue. It was bitter cold. Shmerel dragged his feet through the deep snow as though in a daze. One night, in a dream, he had seen just such a land covered with snow, a sky of the same frosty blue. He had heard a voice coming from the West, calling: "Come to me, Shmerel."

As he tramped through the deep snow, he thought he heard the voice again and again: "Come to me, Shmerel."

Shmerel tramped on. He saw a castle in the distance and walked toward it. Suddenly he heard the cry of a man:

"Out of the depths have I cried unto thee, O my Lord."

Simple Shmerel came closer to the castle. He saw a clump of bare trees, the branches laden with snow. Under the trees there was a little red sentry booth, and near it two soldiers stood on guard. Then he heard the cry again.

"Yea, though I walk through the valley of the shadow of death I will fear no evil, for Thou art with me."

It seemed to come from beneath the earth, beyond the gates of the castle.

Shmerel tried to enter the gates but the two soldiers drew their swords and crossed them in front of him.

"No one can pass!" they said.

Shmerel pushed the swords aside and asked:

"Who is it that prays?"

The sentries became frightened. What kind of man was this who was not afraid of swords?

"A Jew," they answered.

"Where is he?" asked Simple Shmerel.

"Over there in the pit. He was thrown in with his wife and all his children."

"Why?" asked the queer, ragged beggar.

"You'd better go away, old man. If the prince sees us talking with you, he'll hang us from the nearest tree," said the sentries.

"Why was this done?" said Simple Shmerel, with a strange look in his eyes.

"How should we know why the Prince did it?" they answered. "Maybe the Jew didn't pay his taxes or some debt that he owes. Maybe he would not do the bear dance to amuse the Prince and his guests. Who knows?"

"But it's a pity," said Simple Shmerel.

The sentries smiled sadly. "You're a simpleton, old man. You're a simpleton," they said.

Something happened in Shmerel's mind when he heard the word "simpleton." Simpleton. . . . Simple Shmerel, the Holy Man, the worker of miracles. . . . HE was Simple Shmerel, the Holy Man!

Suddenly Shmerel spoke out clear and strong:

"Tell the Prince I want to see him!"

"Are you crazy, old man? We are fathers of families. The Prince would hang us."

"Go to the Prince!" commanded Shmerel, more sternly.

The watchmen were frightened. "But what shall we tell him?" they asked.

"Tell him that Simple Shmerel, the Holy Man, waits to see him."

The watchmen hurried off to the castle and soon came back with a butler.

Shmerel followed the butler. He tapped his staff on the polished floors and soiled the Persian rugs with his wet boots.

Shmerel stood before the Prince. A proud, fierce figure, he commanded:

"Free the Jews!"

"Who are *you* to command *me*?"

"I am Simple Shmerel, the Holy Man."

"A Holy Man!" the Prince exclaimed. "How do *I* know you're a Holy Man?"

"The whole world knows it," answered Shmerel, proudly.

"*I* don't," jeered the Prince. Then he said, mockingly, "I'll see what kind of a miracle man you are! Get down into the courtyard," he ordered. "I'll set my hunting dogs

116

on you. If you escape with your life, it will really be a miracle!"

Shmerel stood there, unafraid.

"Free the Jews, I command you!"

"If you escape, I'll set the Jews free," sneered the Prince.

They went into the courtyard where the Prince kept his pack of hunting dogs. They were as large as wolves and as savage as wild boars. They were so fierce that only the head keeper could handle them. They had been trained to let neither stranger nor beggar come near the castle; at first, the dogs would even jump upon the scarecrows in the gardens, taking them for beggars, and tear the ragged dummies to pieces. But the keeper had taught the dogs not to touch the scarecrows.

Shmerel walked to the center of the yard, leaned on his staff, and calmly waited for the dogs. The Prince unleashed them with his own hands. "Tear him to pieces," shouted the Prince, pointing at Shmerel. The dogs ran swiftly toward him. Shmerel didn't stir. They jumped wildly about him, barking fiercely, but lo and behold— they didn't touch him. *To them he was just another scarecrow.*

The Prince was stunned. He called off the dogs and commanded:

"Set the Jews free."

Shmerel turned and calmly walked out of the yard. He went over the hill and disappeared. Simple Shmerel had worked his last miracle.